THE WANTON WEDGE

THE WANTON WEDGE

by

Robert F. Shreve

A Geneva Book

Carlton Press, Inc.   New York, N.Y.

for Barbara,
who laughs with me

THE WANTON WEDGE

1.

It was as nice an April morning as you're apt to see around Savannah, Georgia, or anywhere else in the world for that matter, but Freddie Flatbelly didn't notice as he wheeled his mature Ford Escort across the causeway to the affluent community called The Soundings on Slipaway Slough. Freddie was deep in thought, and hardly acknowledged the cheery salute the guard threw him as he drew up to the security gate.

"You're running early today, Freddie Boy; and isn't Monday your day off?"

"No rest for the weary, Sam," he said as he slipped into low gear and gunned on past. Freddie was assistant pro at the Oleander course, and wasn't even scheduled to be at the shop today because the whole facility was closed on Mondays, but he had his reasons. His main reason was that the head pro had twice passed him over for a salary increase, and he was seizing the opportunity to get even with that SOB. Not a bad plan, either, surreptitiously adding more lead weight to only the even numbered irons in his boss's bag. Could be just a little problem with swing-rhythm in the tournament at Hilton Head next week.

It was just seven o'clock as he parked the Escort and walked about fifty yards to the shop. As he fumbled for his key to unlock the door, he heard a brief scuffling noise inside which startled him enough to drop the key to the sidewalk. It was a good twenty seconds before he was able to retrieve the key and work up enough nerve to unlock the door and enter.

Then he wished he hadn't. In fact he wished he hadn't even thought of coming in this morning with that hare-brained scheme for revenge he must have dreamed up in a moment of sheer madness. But wishing wouldn't make that body go away. The Corpus Delicti (Freddie had heard it called that on Perry Mason) was

9

sprawled ungracefully between a glass display case and a rack of golf shirts, whose gaudy colors gave a pretty good indication why they were priced at "70% off." The massive bruise on the temple of what had been a handsome face pretty well matched the ugliest mauve shirt on the rack. Just one look was more than enough to send Freddie stumbling to the phone to call Sam at the gate. It didn't take Sam and his boss in Security long to deduce that murder was not mentioned anywhere in their job descriptions, and in due course, Lieutenant B. B. Tolliver of the Violent Crimes Investigation Unit was on the scene.

It's tempting to picture Billy Bob Tolliver as the typical red-necked sheriff caricatured and immortalized on a thousand TV shows, but B.B. was nothing like THAT. Sure, he looked something like *that,* starting with a belly more than formidable enough to keep the slack out of the worn cowhide belt which held up his sagging denims, and working on up past a tobacco-stained black cowboy shirt to a bull neck supporting a multiplicity of jowls. If the stereotype were accurate, B.B. should have had mean little squinty eyes peering with malevolence and suspicion out over a flattened porcine nose. The fact is, his nose was quite regular in size and shape, and was rendered nearly invisible by the astonishingly wide blue eyes exuding innocence and good will, belying the penetrating intelligence which served him so well in his chosen profession.

And it's true that he talked like *that,* at least sometimes he did when he was excited or frustrated or angry or needed to make a point of some kind; disdaining to use just one syllable to pronounce a word when he could add to its richness by stretching it to two. ("Prosperity" to him was "Goo-ud Tie-ums"). But most other times he spake the King's English as well as you or I, but with the soft friendly accent of the deep South.

Four years at the University of Georgia and a couple of courses at the FBI academy had enhanced his natural deductive powers, and it had been my pleasure to work with him on several occasions when an off-beat approach had been necessary to wrap up a particularly tangled murder case.

Lt. Tolliver arrived at the Oleander pro shop about thirty minutes after the call had been received in police headquarters. He nodded to Patrolman Pat Flaherty who was standing guard at the door, and the two of them entered the shop.

"Lieutenant, we got here at 7:22, just twelve minutes ago. That poor soul," (he pointed to Freddy Flatbelly slumped in a chair behind the desk), "was the only one here when we arrived, and we've admitted no one since."

Flaherty paused, uncertain of what to say next. He wasn't used to being involved in a murder case, and he didn't know if there was anything more he should have done.

"That's fine, Pat," Tolliver replied. He had met the young patrolman a couple of times, and liked him. "Has anyone checked to be sure our victim is really dead?"

"Yessir, first thing I did when I got here was check his pulse, and I found none. But I'd feel better if you looked at him yourself."

"Just what I was fixing to do, Pat," Billy Bob assured him, turning toward the spot where the victim lay.

It didn't take the experienced investigator long to verify that the man had indeed departed this vale of tears. He was clad in fashionable golf attire, from his powder blue shirt and pink checked slacks to his chamois-leather golf glove, but was still wearing his street loafers instead of spiked golf shoes. He was lying on the lush green carpet with his body bent to the side and his head twisted grotesquely back, as if he were trying to count his own vertebrae. The huge purple bruise on the temple gave further evidence of the force of the blow which apparently killed him.

"Pat, did anyone call the coroner yet?"

"I don't think so. Should I have done that?"

Billy Bob could see Flaherty's discomfort, and smiled at him. "No, Pat, you've done just fine. Have you questioned the young man over there?"

"Only enough to find out who he is. Name's Fred Flatbelly, and he's assistant golf pro here. He discovered the body."

"OK Pat, please call the coroner and the lab boys. Also the photographer, and tell him to bring his Bi-Lens."

As Flaherty gratefully left the scene to carry out his orders, B.B. walked over to where Freddy was sitting, and sat down next to him.

"Mr. Flatbelly, I'm Lieutenant Tolliver. I guess you've had quite a shock for this early in the morning."

Freddy looked up at the friendly face with the wide blue eyes, and felt marginally better. His gray-green complexion began to take on a little healthier hue, indicating that he just might possibly live.

"Yes sir, it was a terrible shock seeing Mr. Brasher lying there with that terrible wound on his head," Freddy managed to say.

"I take it you recognized him. What's his full name?"

"It's Mr. Barry Brasher, sir. He's a club member and was very active in the golf program," he replied. "He was very good to me," he added, fighting back tears.

Tolliver saw that the young man was moving toward hysteria, and he'd better get as much information as he could now, rather than postpone his interrogation and give Freddy time to figure out what he should and shouldn't tell the police.

"Freddy," Billy Bob said in a soft reassuring voice, "tell me what happened this morning."

"Well sir, I got to the shop exactly at seven, and had just taken my keys out to unlock the door when I heard this noise inside. It did startle me, and I guess I fumbled a little with the key before I managed to unlock the door," he blurted out, and then paused for breath.

"How would you describe the noise?"

"Well, it was like a scuffling sound, then a loud thud, followed by another dull thud, but not as loud as the first."

"Then what?"

"I managed to get the door open, and went in and saw poor Mr. Brasher lying . . . over there." He nodded his head nervously in the direction of the deceased.

"You saw no one else?"

"No, and that was a relief, because somebody had done something awful to Mr. Brasher, and I was really scared."

"How do you suppose that 'somebody' disappeared without you seeing them?"

Freddy sucked in his breath sharply, as he realized for the first time that he might be suspected of doing this terrible thing. "Well, he could have gone out the side door."

The Lieutenant got up from his chair and walked over to the front door, then sighted back toward the shop interior.

"Freddy, with those big glass windows on the front and side walls, it seems like you would have seen anybody leaving through that side door toward the rear."

The young pro was beginning to look desperate as he imagined himself sitting in a dark cell on death row, all because he didn't see someone who must have been there.

"But . . . I know! I was so nervous when I heard the noise inside that I dropped my keys by the door. They fell down between two flagstones and it took me a while to get them out of the crack. That must have been when the murderer escaped!" he finished triumphantly.

Tolliver looked at him speculatively for a moment, and then commented, "Did you stop to think that he may have hidden back there in the bathroom? For that matter he might be there right now, since you haven't seen him leave."

"No sir, I know he's not," he said, and his face began to redden, "You see, after I saw poor Mr. Brasher lying there, I felt kind of sick, and I rushed into the bathroom to throw up. There was no one there, Thank God."

Billy Bob thought this over. He had given Freddy a possible out for not having seen the alleged murderer, and he had not taken it. After a few more questions, the coroner and the lab people showed up, and he dismissed Flatbelly, with a warning not to leave town.

Over the next couple of days Lt. Tolliver interviewed everyone he could find who might have any information on the case, and reviewed all the evidence from the scene of the crime. He quickly deduced that this was not going to be a run-of-the-mill murder case, and began toying with the thought of tapping unorthodox resources, which meant me, Clive Trebor, certified free spirit and part-time sleuth. He as quickly discarded the depressing idea.

But unfortunately this was an election year, and the local press would try to crucify his boss if he didn't come up with some answers fast. Knowing his boss, B.B. figured if it came to a crucifying, Capt. Frost would somehow pull a Barabbas, and one Lt. Billy Bob Tolliver would end up on the cross.

13

He had plenty of leads to follow up, but was getting no answers from the Soundings residents (commonly known as Soundingers), who didn't seem to be on his wave length. With no breakthrough in sight, B.B. gave in to the inevitable, and that still meant me . . . Clive Trebor, 44 hard years old, with a mere 170 lbs of gristle on a six-foot-one frame, trying hard to hide too many anxieties behind a bland visage adorned with a go-to-hell mustache. The piercing eyes and thin lips could remind you of Clint Eastwood intoning, "Dying ain't much of a living, boy!" but the whole effect was soon spoiled by that lock of straight black hair falling without warning down across the long forehead, breaking the spell.

If you're one of those nasty people who tend to criticize and minimize the other guy's enterprise, the sight of Clive Trebor and B.B. Tolliver on the scene of a crime might remind you of Laurel and Hardy, except that in our case the mustache was on the skinny one. But unlike old Stan and Ollie, we had always been able to hack our way through the underbrush of criminal obfuscation and emerge with the Grail of pure TRUTH, usually only slightly tarnished with compromise.

2.

B.B.'s call couldn't have come at a better time. I had been making a reasonable living the past several years at various clubs around Palm Springs in the California desert at what I regard as intelligent betting on the links, (although I know a few disgruntled losers who have used the ugly word "hustler").

Then calamity struck. I could still split the fairway out maybe 265, and my irons were as crisp as ever, high and true, with enough backspin to check up on concrete. But some sort of insidious malady had crept into my putting game and reduced it to dreck. Sam Snead, or whoever, was right when he said putting is the curse of the golfing class. Only six months ago I was sinking 15-foot sidehill putts to collect large green ones from wealthy snowbirds, who paid better than they played. Now I was the patsy, missing easy four-footers for serious piles of pesos. The only compensation was that I started getting invited to play at all the better clubs in The Springs, and even on down the Valley as far as Bermuda Dunes.

As my stroke decayed, I began to try anything that might help. First I decided that my equipment was the problem. I began to try long shafts and short shafts, long blades and stubby ones, heavy and light, black and white, silver and gold, new and old. Even tried one called "Bassackwards," which performed about as you would expect. I investigated materials of construction ranging from hickory to plexiglass to carefully selected fibers of Rocky Mountain oysters. The only effective equipment change I ran across involved stripping off the bottom three inches of the grip to get the advantage when using the "within the leather" convention for conceding putts.

Next I went to one of the most famous golf teachers in the Valley (who shall be nameless to avoid legal action). He taught me three different awkward stances, each more ludicrous than the one before. He also taught me that the grain always runs toward Indio. Now everybody KNOWS that, but it usually just isn't true: it often runs toward some recently-flooded date palm orchard nearby. And the last thing this licensed wizard taught was PLUMB-BOBBING, wherein one holds the putter with two fingers in front of the face and sights along the shaft. Although this maneuver purports to determine the slope of the green along the intended path of the ball, few golfers realize that it was originated by the terrible-tempered Tommy Bolt, who was only checking to see if the shaft was bent after his last club-throwing episode.

About then I was desperate enough to visit a Sports Psychologist, one Les Zents, M.D. & Ph.D. (I think he had a third degree, but I've never been too enthusiastic about third degrees.) This particular shrink had a rather unique approach to curing ailing putting strokes: he tried to get you to understand the formidable forces you were up against in mastering the art. He started by discussing the derivation of the word "putt." He quoted some semanticists who believe it derived from the Latin verb *"putare,"* meaning "to think so but not be sure;" or maybe the German adjective *"putzig"* which translates as "queer, quaint or droll." Other possible sources are the German noun *"putzfrau"* meaning someone engaged in unskilled labor; or "putter" indicating a "turkey." (How many times have you heard that word around the

15

green?) And lastly he pointed out the good old American expression "puttering around," which involves aimless motion in which little is accomplished.

Similarly (he explained), the putting venue, the green, is always treated negatively, even in the USGA Rules of Golf. For example, Rule 19-1 refers to "the rub of the green," which means "if something bad happens to your ball, it's just tough luck, buddy." The well-known linksman Will Shakespeare, who carried a 13 handicap at the challenging Stratford-on-Avon course, referred to this when he wrote, "Aye, there's the rub!"

Up to this point I could buy what the good doctor was saying, but then he over-reached. He proceeded to tell me that the green is part of a Satanic universe ruled over by the Green Goddess, an eminence so foul that a particularly noxious salad dressing was named for her. He backed this up by citing the case of a professional golfer named Hubert Harddriver, whose putting ability bordered on the mediocre. In his many attempts at improvement he ended up in a posture like that of a tall man whose vest is secured to the bottom button of his fly. Then in a dream brought on by consuming too many green creme-de-menthes at the 19th hole, the answer was given to him. He immediately changed his name to Hubert Green, began wearing only green clothing, and otherwise acted to appease the deities of the Green. His immediate success is well documented. In my desperate condition I was ready to grasp at even so outlandish a straw as this, but I checked around with a few of the boys who are connected, and found, to my disgust, that Hubert Green had never ever been named Harddriver, and in fact, didn't even like green creme-de-menthe.

I continued to search for my lost putting stroke, and continued to donate to every linksman lucky enough to get me into a game, until a little incident occurred in the locker room at La Quinta: I got thrown out bodily for welching on a bet. Licking my wounds, I retreated to my rented room back in the Springs and took stock. My creditors had impounded my clubs to settle my outstanding bets, and everything else of value had become the property of Paddy's Pawn Palace. What I had left were a couple of changes of clothing, a battered putter which had betrayed me, and of course the Hupmobile Skylark Custom. As my fortunes had worsened, I gradually let everything go except the old Hup. It was built in 1940, as the old Hupp Brothers Motor Co made a last-gasp attempt at survival by acquiring the body dyes, and therefore the styling, of the 1937 Cord. When they named it the "Custom," they meant just that: no two were finished alike, and mine was one of the finest. It was a jewel then, and had only gotten better with age; it was still one of the few cars that could turn heads in this land of the gold-plated Rolls.

Without any real plan, I loaded up the trunk of the car, paid my overdue rent with the last of my cash, and headed south on 111. I was still boiling as I rassled the old laminated-cherry steering wheel into a sharp turn onto Rte. 74, headed for San Diego. As I crossed El Paseo, I hit that deep-throated horn a couple of toots in farewell to the sweet life. Then I double-clutched her roughly into 2nd gear, and began to gain speed as I headed up the long incline and into the first of the switchbacks scaling the side of the mountain. I wasn't sure where I was going, but I hoped that wherever it was, they'd never heard of the ugly game of golf.

About two thousand feet up the side of the mountain I pulled off at that big scenic overlook for a last view of all the places that had been so damned much fun before they put out UNWELCOME mats with my name tastefully inscribed thereon. I was struck by an amusing whim: I'd often seen those crazy hang-gliders take off from this spot, and circle for hours before coming to a gentle landing on the valley floor far below. I opened the trunk of the Hup, and extracted that bruised putter, the last vestige of a life gone to ruin. I went over to the edge and drew my arm back into launching position, at the same time intoning, "Let's see how far *you* can glide, you sonavabitch!"

But before I could complete the dirty deed, a quiet voice behind me said simply, "I wouldn't do that."

I whirled around to confront the ghost of Walter Hagen! Then as my nerves unjangled, I saw that it really wasn't a ghost, but an old gent in plus-fours, argyle sweater, 1935 golf cap, and bow tie. He wasn't quite Walter Hagen, and he sure as hell wasn't Payne Stewart.

As I recovered, he reached out and gently took the offending object from my hand. "My boy," he said, "I'm Phineas Physis and I can tell you authoritatively that there are no bad putters, only bad putterers."

17

Although I agreed with this profundity at least 98%, I couldn't see that it was going to help my disposition *or* my finances one whole hell of a lot.

Obviously reading my thoughts, he withdrew from his pocket a slightly scuffed Titleist. With his foot he smoothed a path in the soft dirt beside the pavement, and stuck a tee at one end. Then, with *my* putter, which hadn't sunk a putt of more than five feet in the last millenium, he propelled the ball over bumps and depressions to come to rest snugly against that tee. Lucky shot, of course.

Again reading my puny mind, the stranger replied, "Very little luck was involved. Behold."

Whereupon he proceeded about thirty feet up and across the rough pavement, and with the greatest delicacy putted that ball down the slope whereupon it softly kissed the tee. Without further delay he obtained the same result from various positions up, down, left and right of the target.

You don't have to smite me with a shillelagh. With all my being I wanted to know his secret. I lusted after it. I had to have it.

Anticipating my question, the old gent replied, "I'll teach you how for a small price."

Anything, anything. But I had no cash.

"Not to worry. Just turn over the title to that old car you're driving and I'll teach you everything."

Now I knew how Eve felt when the serpent offered her that deal in the Garden of Eden. It was wrong. No way could I give up the old Hup. But a vision of me putting like that again was too strong. We shook hands on it.

"It's very simple," he said. "As a retired physiologist, I've been working on an unusual project to pass the time. I discovered that the muscle which controls the putting stroke, the Putteus Maximus, has strong neural connections to the jawbone. Ergo, to make a putt go right or left merely skew the mouth in the proper direction. For a long putt, hold the mouth wide open as if shouting; and for a little downhill dribbler, purse the lips in a simulated whisper. Simple maybe, but profound. And if you find that you are still overshooting or undershooting the hole, remember the comment of the ancient Tibetan yak-driver, explaining his erratic progress through the Himalayas, 'Uphill is slow; downhill is fast.'"

I couldn't believe it was so easy, but I made long putts from all over that parking lot. I turned over the title to the Hupmobile to Dr. Physis, and he gave me a ride back to the valley.

Within seven days I'd won a '73 Ford Fairlane and $250 in cash at the Rattlesnake Gulch Municipal nine the other side of Twenty-nine Palms. But although my golf game was back, I was still Persona-very-Non-Grata in these parts. I pointed the Fairlane's battered nose East.

3.

B.B. had somehow tracked me down in Atlanta, where the Fairlane's health had taken a serious turn for the worse. He allowed as how he had an opportunity for me to do something worthwhile and enjoyable and make a fair piece of change doing it. His department had a discretionary budget to handle unusual needs, and he had easily convinced his boss that, in an election year, solving this murder real quick was an unusual need. I would receive a daily "consulting fee" plus reasonable expenses. I had a feeling that it was going to be tough to prove that *any* expenses I could think of would be considered "reasonable," but right now I didn't have a real plethora of job offers, and that daily fee looked good. I agreed to take the Greyhound out of Atlanta if he would meet me at the bus station in Savannah late that night. He would be only too happy to.

But what with the bus limping in three hours late, the vending machine in the station being out of boiled peanuts, and the coffee damn near iced over, that "only too happy to" had gone down hill by the time he greeted me in Savannah.

"Shee-it, man, why caint you drive to town like most decent folks? Ah've been freezing my ay-uss in this cow shed half the night."

"It's good to see you too, Billy Bob."

"Oh hell, Cli-uv, it is good to see you," as his big blue eyes regained their sparkle, "It's just that I hate cold coffee and waiting for Yankees."

19

I accepted this as an apology, but still felt that I had a point to make. "B.B., I could have had the Fairlane fixed, but I figured it might be useful to assume the role of a new resident of The Soundings, and I didn't think a 1973 Ford would be normal transportation for the role."

"Cli-uv, you're mighty right. Ah don't recollect seeing none of those Soundingers driving a '73 anything."

We had arrived at a satisfactory understanding. He needed me but wasn't going to be subservient; and he had unconsciously trotted out the broad accent that told me we were on his home turf. On other occasions the exaggerated drawl might disappear, and I would have further interpreting to do. But that was later and this was now, so we got into the big police cruiser which had been resting in a No Parking zone for the past three hours, and powered on up Abercorn to The Kettle for hot coffee, fried ham and grits.

After B.B. narrowly averted starvation by polishing off seconds and thirds of everything, he began to fill me in on the progress of his investigation, describing the abundance of clues he had found at the scene of the crime.

"There's a couple other things bothering me, Clive," Billy Bob added, and the sho-nuff accent had disappeared.

"Like what?"

"Like what was Brasher doing in the pro shop so early on a Monday morning when the shop and the course were closed for the day?"

"Hard to say," I offered unhelpfully.

"And how did he get in? You reckon somebody gave him a key? If so, who and why?"

"Lots of possibilities," I replied brilliantly.

B.B. looked at me like 'why did I call this clown,' but he continued, "And maybe the biggest question is how he got out without being seen. If, as young Mr. Flatbelly told it, he heard a scuffle just before he entered, is it likely that the assailant could have escaped without being seen?"

"B.B., there is a possible answer to your questions—Freddie himself could have done the dirty deed. He could have arranged to have Brasher meet him there on some trumped up excuse; as for the rest, we have only his word about a struggle and an escaping assailant."

Tolliver's facial expression told me eloquently that he was not too enthusiastic about having an idiot as his partner on this case. Then he breathed a sigh, and intoned slowly, "Clive, it will please you to know that I have already investigated this possibility, and have nearly eliminated Flatbelly from the list of suspects."

"B.B., I wasn't intimating that you hadn't done your job. But would you mind sharing your reasoning with a tired old Yankee who didn't get a helluva lot of shuteye on the damn bus from Atlanta?"

"Apology accepted, Clive," and he grinned at me. "First of all the young assistant pro didn't seem to have any motive for the slaying; in fact several members stated that the two were friends, and as Chairman of the Golf Facilities Committee Brasher had put in a good word for Freddie on several occasions. But there is another reason, too."

"And what might that be, Oh Exalted Genius?"

"The most important reason is that my highly trained nose tells me young F. Flatbelly is not the type to commit this kind of crime."

With anyone else I would have laughed out loud at this ridiculous statement, but in all my association with Tolliver, I had never known his hunches proven wrong.

"Here's the coroner's report, Clive. As we expected, the blow to the head killed the victim, but we did learn that he had sustained a fractured left wrist and a sprained right ankle. I guess you can attribute them to the struggle which must have taken place."

Normally in a situation like this several suspects would be identified, but B.B. had had little success in putting the finger on individuals who might fit the trail the murderer had left behind.

Tolliver said, "I'm pretty sure some of those fat cats aren't telling me everything they know. That's why I called you. I figured with you being born with a silver spoon in your mouth and all, you'd have a whole lot better chance than I in loosening a few tongues."

I accepted B.B.'s assessment. "Like I said earlier, I think our best bet is for me to actually become a resident, a Soundinger, and work my way into the confidence of the residents and club staff."

"No problem with that, Clive. But listen old buddy, make it as short and sweet as you can, because my lovable old boss Capt. Frost is taking a lot of heat. Now we don't want him to be upset, do we?"

I got the message, and would do everything I could to save Billy Bob's job. I shifted my 16-cylinder brain into overdrive to puzzle out how to become *one of them* posthaste.

B.B. drove me to the nearest car-rental agency where I signed a one-month lease on a late model Caddy. It wasn't my Hupmobile, but it beat hell out of shoe-horning my lanky frame into one of those foreign heaps with the kidney-busting ride and the exaggerated price tag. I threw my duffle bag into the trunk and headed for the Soundings.

As I drove southeast from the historic city of Savannah and crossed the causeway spanning the salt marsh, my first impression of the island was that the Garden of Eden could well have been here. God must have been in a good mood when he placed all the lovely old live-oaks, magnolias, palms and pines in harmony, and Man for once had declined to spoil it. To the natural flora had been added dogwood and redbud and great profusions of azaleas, as well as an infinite variety of flowers and shrubs surrounding each dwelling. All of the winding streets were lined with plantings, and a number of stands of trees and bushes had been left in their natural state, to be enjoyed forever by the residents and their lucky guests.

Where Man's hand was most evident, in the residences, clubhouses, golf courses and bicycle paths, restraint had been the watchword. I learned that architectural covenants had been drawn up outlawing garish colors and unsightly designs, and a vigilant citizenry made sure that nothing unpleasing to the eye was allowed to appear.

As for the residents, they scrupulously avoided ostentation; they were almost aggressive in their humility, and gladly paid for their good fortune by supporting every worthy charitable or cultural cause in the Savannah metropolitan area.

It was an integrated community, if by "integrated" you mean a mixture of doctors and lawyers, stockbrokers and executives, young and old, wealthy and almost-wealthy, Southerners and Yankees, Republicans and Democrats (a few), white and black (a few).

The residents felt at home within the guarded gates of their enclave, where they frustrated themselves on six championship golf courses or sustained sprains and contusions at the three tennis centers, and they had to journey but a few miles to Savannah to take advantage of all its facilities and cultural attractions. Completing the picture of community harmony, native Savannahians were happy to offer fair value for the substantial daily inflow of Yankee dollars. To paraphase T. Oglethorpe Beaufort, "We don't mind the carpet-bags as long as they're filled with gold."

This bright Spring Day luck was with me, and I was able to rent a Condo and join the Club before Old Sol made a spectacular exit behind the palms lining the west marsh. My next step was to get my hands on a copy of the local press, which turned out to be a glossy weekly called "The Soundinger Humdinger." This magazine was much better than the name it had been saddled with, and was dedicated to satisfying the informational needs of the Soundings on Slipaway Slough. It was in these pages that I found a biography of one of the residents, a lucky stroke which provided a possible strategy for quickly integrating into the community. A little discreet questioning at the club bar revealed that such biographies were a frequent feature in the magazine, and a visit to the island library produced enough back issues for me to find a pattern in these well-written pieces.

It seems that most of the subjects written about shared common characteristics: they were truly exciting and successful individuals from the population of interesting people who inhabited the island. Typically, they had risen from humble beginnings to excel in Business, Academia, the Military, Sports, or the Arts. Usually they could leap tall buildings in a single bound, and they had done it all while maintaining true humility. In fact, if they weren't inhibited by Erudition and Couth, they'd probably say, "Shucks, twarn't nothing!" pretty regularly.

In analyzing these factors that led to recognition—Hardship in childhood, Accomplishments in school, and Success in one or more professions—I figured that with a little creativity I could maybe

23

show that I had qualified in all the major areas of notable achievement, and more. My strategy, then, was obvious: I would have my biography published, ensuring recognition in the community, and providing rapid entry into local society. With that thought firmly in mind, I long-handed on the back of an envelope the facts which I could flesh out into a resume for immortality, being careful to cover only the years before I dropped out of conventional society and into the world of golf adventurer and part-time detective:

HARDSHIP IN CHILDHOOD: I had steak but twice a week and made do with lambchops or chicken otherwise. Walked a full block to schoolbus stop when chauffeur was off duty. Ate ordinary chocolate when Truffles unavailable. Didn't wear clothes from Brooks Brothers until fifth grade.

ACCOMPLISHMENTS IN SCHOOL: Was very good at typing. Passed Algebra both years I was in the tenth grade. Leadership recognized by election as Deputy Assistant Scribe of graduating class. Also was voted most likely to outgrow acne.

MILITARY SERVICE: Distinguished service during the war, culminating in award of Good Conduct Medal with Barracks Bag Cluster. Ranked in top ten in Stenographers Pool at Fort Issi, Mo. Responsible for uncovering the PX scandal, resulting in demotion of two PFC's. Separated from service with a Fairly Honorable Discharge.

SPORTS: Student manager of football team that went to regional semifinals in Condor, S.C. Played right wing on the fifth line of Southwest Florida University icehockey team, and was red-shirted on lacrosse team of this same powerhouse sports institution. Was never charged by the NCAA with accepting illegal athletic scholarship money.

BUSINESS CAREER: Started at the bottom in family firm, and worked up to Ass't. Vice-president. Was invaluable in training my niece before she assumed the presidency. Contributions were recognized by the Board of Directors, who rewarded me by granting full retirement at age thirty-five.

SCIENTIFIC ACHIEVEMENTS: Discovered Penicillin (repeatedly). Invented and developed new product "Windshield Wipers For

Eyeglasses." Marketed same. Closed out project with gratifying tax write-off.

THE ARTS: Introduced Belly-button Lint Macrame' in Public Housing Projects. Author of "Arcane & Absurd: A Fresh Look At The Ampersand." Sponsored the Robert E. Lee Charity Ball in the south side of Chicago, Ill., and chaired the damage-control committee following this event.

What had seemed like a possibility when lying there unorganized in my fluid mind, didn't hold up to the acid test of the written word. I balled up the paper and made a three-point bank shot off the wall into the waste basket.

Maybe my biography would have been interesting enough to be accepted for publication if I'd been able to include the last nine years of my life, but that would have blown my cover. Still, my life did divide rather neatly into two distinct parts: 35 years wasted on a dull and proper existence, followed by almost a decade of living on the edge.

I had been doomed to wimpism at birth by my mother. My Dad, God love him, had his heart set on naming me Robert Aka Trebor, the palindrome appealing to his poetic nature, and the initials a subtle rebuff to Mother's overbearing sense of propriety. But Mumsy was appalled, and insisted on a name which would be dignified and proper and as English as Tea and Crumpets, (although all of her ancestors were Eastern European). So "Clive" I came to be, and a proper upbringing went with it. Dear Mother had achieved wealth when she married Dad and the family business, and now she would experience social stature through her only child.

It turned out to be more of a chore than she had anticipated. I wasn't openly rebellious, although I hated every situation she placed me in. It was just that I had a natural aversion for confrontation, and a pretty formidable talent for subterfuge. Indeed, if Haversham Military Academy, to whom Mumsy entrusted her teenage son for a proper education, had given awards for such things, I would have been Sneak-of-the-Week scores of times. For example, we were taught the manly art of fisticuffs by a retired English Army major, who had reputedly been champion of his regiment during the Boer War or such. The way the major taught

25

boxing, it seemed more like a minuet, with fluffy oversized mittens laced to the wrists, dancing about with fists held high, throwing an occasional feint, and rarely launching even the semblance of a real punch. I figured that if you were going to hit someone you should do it as quickly and efficiently as possible, ruling out the opportunity for your opponent to hit back. Therefore, I avoided this class whenever possible, and took advantage of the time to learn real mayhem from one of the school's Japanese gardeners, who went by the single name of Otsuki. In exchange for a rather large portion of my allowance each month, Otsuki taught me basic Judo, along with a number of variations which would get you thrown out of any respectable Martial Arts Club in the U.S.A. *or* Japan. Not only was I talented sneak-wise, but I seemed uncommonly adept at rendering an opponent defenseless so quickly that a real confrontation never got off the ground. My training with Otsuki continued for nearly two years, until I was at least as skilled as he, and no longer willing to shell out the money I now needed to save for more pressing needs, like Dates With Girls.

But over a long period of years, Mother did wear me down, and I was fulfilling most of her ambitions at the Club, at the right social events, and even as a so-called executive at the family firm. So she seemed to have it made on all fronts. Then, during the year of my thirty-fifth birthday, things went to hell in a handbasket. Old Dad had finally had enough, and dropped out of the whole scene. Dropping out with him was his young and shapely secretary, and where they dropped to was a condo at Treasure Cay beach on Abaco in the Bahamas. Shortly thereafter his companion shipped out with a sun-tanned stud who was about thirty years younger than Dad, in a boat with about 900 more horses than pater's sturdy Boston Whaler. Apparently this didn't do anything real great for my father's ego or his disposition, and he was last seen gunning that whaler out of the harbour, a full load of gasoline and 4 cases of Old Methusalem dark rum aboard. No one has heard from him since. As a consequence of this, by contractural arrangement the family business reverted entirely to my uncle Julius and his progeny. Perhaps Mother could have endured the shame, but the loss of the bulk of the money was too much, and within a year her troubled heart just said the hell with it.

So there I was, probably an orphan, with little money and no skill except a knack for really nasty self defense, and one other thing: I could hit a golf ball long and straight consistently. I had compensated for years of frustration in business by spending more and more hours on the links, and was rewarded by seeing my handicap pass through the lower digits on down to zero and beyond.

At about this time I met Fiona Feather at a Charity Ball for the benefit of mistreated Pomeranians. The cumulative numbness of spirit which these affairs engender over an hour or two propelled me out to the veranda where one could carry his liquid refreshment and experience reasonable quiet and a little fresh air. I damn near bumped into Fiona, similarly laden and with the same mission in mind.

A little polite conversation quickly revealed how very alike we were. I don't mean physically alike; while I'm tall and thin, and have never been accused of looking like an athlete, Fiona was one of those rare women who managed to look tanned and healthy and athletic, but at the same time had enough curves on her five-foot-six frame to rate a second glance wherever she went. She wasn't a striking beauty like one or two I've known, but when her big warm smile kicked in and lit up her features, she could make a eunuch forget what he was. The only physical attributes we shared were dark brown eyes and very black hair.

But we did have a lot in common. Just as I, she had been named in the best Jolly Old England fashion, and brought up by a social-climbing mother. Incredibly, she was also a scratch golfer whose game always turned up a notch or two when enough chips were on the line. And as a last coincidence, she had recently suffered separation from family and fortune. We hit it off right away, left the Ball together, and began seeing each other constantly. We even began teaming up on the golf course, providing companionship and instruction to vacationing couples, and exacting fair payment by judicious betting and the sinking of clutch putts.

But I digress. My biography, lacking the more interesting nine years of my life, was residing in the waste basket, and I would have to find other ways to penetrate society at the Soundings.

Being only 30% abashed by this turn of events, I contacted Lt. Tolliver and agreed to meet him at Pearl's Elegant Pelican for a bowl of She Crab Soup and some heavy strategizing.

Following the delicious soup and a great broiled grouper, washed down with an Anchor Steam, B.B. urged me to pick up the pace of the investigation, as several reporters and a couple of layers of bosses were breathing down his neck. "Cli-uv," he said, his agitation bringing back the hushpuppy accent, "they're on me like stink on shee-it. We've got to quit drag-assing and get in frigging gear."

"Shee-it yourself," I imitated his accent, "My ay-uss has been in every frigging gear I can find."

"Sorry Clive, I'm just getting up-tight," he said soberly. "What say we go over all the physical evidence we've got first, then draw up a list of possible suspects."

"Sounds good. Then I can zero in on each one, and try to find a way to interview them without arousing suspicion. You know, B.B., all that work I've been doing with my 'clients' on the Links has equipped me for this diplomatic task you've assigned me," I added, trying to keep a straight face.

Billy Bob winced. He always disapproved of my golf gambling, and didn't like to hear about it even in jest. He changed the subject.

"OK, let's get on with the physical evidence," he said hurriedly.

He pulled out a large stack of photo blow-ups taken at the scene of the crime. Modern police photography is a marvel to behold, and B.B.'s portfolio on this case was about as impressive as any I'd ever seen. I was particularly pleased to see that some of the shots had been taken with the new wide angle Bi-Lens which produced a three dimensional effect.

"Here's the victim," B.B. drawled, "We later identified him as Soundings resident and Club member Barry Brasher, age 42."

I examined the photo Tolliver handed me, and noted that the victim could have been a picture out of those upscale magazines I was used to seeing in Palm Springs, where Golf is king. Even his golf glove was two-toned pink and blue, and he would have looked like one of those fashion models if someone hadn't taken a divot out of his handsome features with some sort of deadly weapon. I soon found out what that weapon was when B.B. handed me several close ups of the wound. It exhibited a surface pattern strikingly similar to the face of a golf club, or at least to that part of the club face which had made violent contact. Even the golf-ignorant B.B. Tolliver had immediately identified the nature of the murder weapon.

"I assume you haven't found the weapon?" I asked.

"Nosir, the perpetrator must have taken it with him. We haven't even found out where the club came from. With the help of the Head Pro, we went over all those shiny new clubs along the wall there, and none of the sets are missing a club, nor was there any visible evidence that any of them was the murder weapon. There is one little catch, though."

"What's that?"

"You see that barrel of wedges and putters over by the wall? The Pro says it may be missing one club. The computer inventory software has been acting up, and he couldn't be sure. He'll let me know when and if they get it straightened out."

"B.B., I hope so, but my experience with computer inventories is that most of the screwing up is done by the operator and not the poor machine. Anyway, what else do we have?"

"Look at these shots of the big glass case," offered B.B., "why didn't it get smashed, considering how close it is to where Brasher must have been cold-cocked?"

Indeed it was some sort of miracle that this large fragile merchandise display case wasn't shattered by the club which had written finis to a very bad day for Mr. Brasher.

Another set of interesting photos had been taken of the thick green carpet which had been the victim's last resting place. These included close-ups of odd marks presumably made by Mr. Brasher's loafers, along with numerous cleat marks of unknown origin. Tolliver had thoughtfully made duplicates of all the photos for my later examination. Then he produced Xeroxes of some papers found in the victim's oversize wallet. These fell into the classification of THINGS TO INVESTIGATE FURTHER WHEN ALL ELSE FAILS. And that's just what I decided to do after we parted ways that evening.

29

4.

Among the papers found in Brasher's pocket were various brief articles, editorials and letters to the editor regarding the deer situation on the island. It appeared that, in common with many other East Coast communities, Slipaway Slough was experiencing a cervine population explosion. The situation had become quite emotional, with some people advocating feeding the animals, while others favored thinning the herds by controlled hunting. It was obvious that Barry Brasher was caught up in this issue, judging from the amount of underlining and peppering of exclamation points throughout the written material found on his person. Seemed to me like a good place to uncover a motive for the slaying.

I had spent the previous evening making friends at the Oleander bar, by judiciously buying more than my share of straight whiskies and the like, so it was to this newly-established "library" that I now headed in search of knowledge.

My modus operandi was to smoothly shift the conversation from the new handicap system or whatever, to the subject of deer. But I seemed to meet with unspoken resistance, as if no one wanted to open this can of worms. This required a more aggressive approach, which I now employed. To get the ball rolling, I decided to give my solution to the problem. Actually, I felt it was quite straightforward, and couldn't understand why others hadn't already proposed it.

"My friends," I addressed the barflies assembled, "the key is this: We have been fencing the deer IN instead of OUT! If you've been paying attention to anything other than those bikinis at the Oleander pool, you will have noticed that our community is virtually surrounded by fence, with practically the only egress through the security gates. Do you think that all those little four-hoofed darlings really want to stay within the boundaries of the Soundings? It may be great for humans, but look at it from the deer's vantage point: they can't own the property or belong to the club or drive a Mercedes, the wildflowers are gone, and most of the tasty morsels left are booby-trapped with enough voltage to discourage the casual browser." I paused to let this profundity sink in.

Finkley spoke up, "You may be right about that, Trebor, but what good does that do?"

Well at least I'd gotten a response. "What good it does is this: knowing the problem, we can easily devise a solution. At a few selected spots, where the fence line is in little wooded areas, we construct special one-way 'gates' for those who wish to vacate the premises. These gates could be designed like reverse lobster traps, or (for you plumbers) check valves: easy to get out, but impossible to get back in again."

I got a few grudging sounds of approval, but Larry Lachrimose complained, "I don't think any plan is worth two cents when we don't even know how many deer are on the Island. That air survey was a farce. The first time they counted 200, and the second time it was 300. I don't trust either count."

"I don't blame you," I said, "but I can assure you the second count was right. This is what happened: they used a special radar having a resolution of 2.5 nano-microns (a measurement pioneered by Prof. David Dawdleson of the Romerly Tower Observatory). This is sufficiently sensitive to detect the color, size and sex of Lyme-bearing ticks on the fur of any varmint below. Furthermore, the radar beam travels at speeds exceeding 1.3 trillion furlongs per fortnight, fast enough to freeze any motion of the target. Having studied science things in school, I am very familiar with how these devices work, and I can deduce what happened on the first aerial survey: There are six positions on the control dial of this particular radar, and the operator inadvertently set it on the 'Squirrel' position instead of the 'Deer' position. So he ended up counting approximately 200 squirrels instead of the 300 deer count he got the second time around."

I thought I had made a brilliant presentation, and that my logic had been faultless, but nobody jumped up on a barstool and shouted, "Ole!" Group lockjaw seemed to set in, and everyone drifted off to handle other more urgent affairs. Everyone, that is, except a very large redheaded citizen of the female persuasion who could obviously hold up the distaff point of view in any cultural exchange. Of course I had noticed her earlier: you don't just overlook the Build-of-the Century when it's giving you the barroom ogle. I mean she was seeworthy from upper deck to keel, with stops along the way. Her soft smooth skin didn't detract one

31

millimicron from the sensational auburn hair which framed her perfect oval face. Although everything was large economy size, it was all so perfectly proportioned that you didn't think of her as being at least six foot-oh in her black net stockings unless you considered arm-wrestling her or such, in which case you'd do well to say "Please" first. But I did find it hard to believe what the bar denizens were saying about her having the hots for my scrawny frame. Mr. Animal Magnetism I'm not.

At any rate, here we were, just she and I, (or maybe her and me), and before I could decide what in the world I was going to do, she moved over to the stool next to mine, and laid a smile on me that melted the wax in both ears, causing a pleasant dizzy feeling that I didn't want to lose too fast.

I guess it was up to me to say something about then, but I was too hypnotized by her emerald green eyes looking into my semi-bloodshot ones to speak or move.

Fortunately she wasn't as paralyzed as I. "I'm Dorothy La-Moste," she said in a husky voice that was pure Peggy Lee.

As in a trance I murmured, "Do you sing?"

She laughed at my immediate embarrassment, and it wasn't in derision, but rather a nice hearty musical laugh that said it was okay and weren't we going to have fun. That broke the ice, and I almost was in control of my faculties again.

"I know you're Clive Trebor, and I've wanted to meet you since I first saw you here. I'm glad the others have left so we can talk; aren't you glad too?"

Now that was a view I had no trouble agreeing to, and I said as much. We began talking trivia about the weather, and then her golf game.

"I just started six months ago and I have my handicap down to twenty, but Charlie (the head pro) says it will go much lower when I learn to pitch and putt."

"I'll bet you hit the ball real well," was all I could think of to say.

She giggled. "Yes, Charlie says I hit the ball farther than any woman he has ever given lessons to. I'm big and strong, I guess; it comes from my mother's side of the family."

I started to say something to the effect that there are lots of big and strong people who can't hit the ball very far and that she must have athletic ability, but a noisy group came piling through the door and up to the bar, drowning out any pearls of wisdom I was about to cast.

Dorothy wrinkled her nose in a frown. "Clive, we can't talk here very well now. How about coming over to my townhouse?" Then she giggled and said, "I might even have some cookies and milk for you, laddie."

I've never been what you call a Chaser, and I never even looked at another woman when Fiona and I were together; but Fiona was long gone, and I could use a little pleasant companionship. Heck, part of my strategy was to integrate into the community, and what better way than cookies and milk with one of the locals? At that point my conscience whispered in my ear, "Come off it, Trebor. You lust after this big beautiful doll and you know it."

Dorothy's townhouse was decorated in what you could call Show Girl Pink. I refrained from asking her if she ever danced in the Follies, (Paris or Las Vegas), but noted with pleasure that she had the long legs and proliferation of tasteful curves to make her a natural. She poured herself a DuBonnet, which I later found to be *her* standard, and a Wild Turkey for me, always a standard in *my* book. There were several vacant chairs, but she chose to snuggle up to me on the love-seat 'to get comfy'.

"How long have you been at the Sounding?" she asked, the husky voice caressing my eardrums as if she was asking something deep and dark and delicious.

"Just a few days," I managed to reply, feeling like a teenager on his first hot date, and thankful that my voice didn't go high and squeaky like a teenager's might.

"Where did you come from?"

I barely suppressed the urge to say the stork brought me, summoned up all of the legendary Trebor cool, and went into my carefully rehearsed cover story. "I just moved from Palm Springs. I'm a golf equipment consultant."

"You should find plenty to do here," the Voice intoned, "with all the golf courses at The Soundings and at Hilton Head. I hope that means you'll be around for a long time." Before I could make any kind of clever reply, she began to nibble my earlobe. I'd heard about earlobe-nibbling somewhere before, but I'd never actually experienced it, and I guess I over-reacted. I jumped up and went over to her portable bar and poured myself a stiff bourbon.

Dorothy looked at me with astonishment and concern.

"Golly, Clive, I'm sorry. I didn't know you were married."

"No, I'm not. Hell I'm not even engaged . . ." I stammered, "It's just that you caught me by surprise, and you're so . . . ," I trailed off in embarrassment.

"Well I have been told that I'm so . . ., but it's nice hearing it from you," she said with that reassuring laugh. "Come on back over here and sit down again."

I did as I was told. She began asking me all kinds of questions, the whole time twisting my forelock of straight black hair playfully with her long red-lacquered forefinger. The effect was like the hypnotist swinging a watch on a chain in front of the subject, telling him that he was getting very sleepy. It was a good thing I'd memorized that cover story, or there's no telling what I might have told her. Pretty soon the deep breathing started, accompanied by at least a normal amount of kissing and caressing. When she took me by the hand and led me toward the bedroom, I knew that was where she was going to serve whatever she meant by "cookies and milk."

Next morning over a cup of steaming Java, Dorothy filled me in on the whole deer controversy, and particularly on the late Mr. Brasher's role in it.

"Honey, old Barry just loved to feed the deer, and he said we ought to let them be fruitful and multiply."

"But suppose they ate all your prize African violets?"

"Well Barry said, 'Just remember, they were here first.' I know a lot of folks didn't agree with him."

"Did any of those folks get violent about it?" I asked in my patented nonchalant interrogation mode.

"Well," Dorothy said, as if concentrating on the answer to an examination question she wasn't really sure of, "most of them were perfect ladies and gentlemen." Then she thought a little harder and a 100-watt bulb turned on in her brain, lighting up the beautiful face with the joy of mental accomplishment. "The worst one of all was that horrid Professor Corkney Clatter."

I guessed that Corkney wasn't even in the top 100 on her favorite persons list. More to the point, she had witnessed a hot exchange between Messrs. Brasher and Clatter, ending with the latter describing in lurid detail what he was going to do to the former.

"He meant to kill him," Dorothy said with a shudder of fear or revulsion.

She had practically painted a sign on the noble Professorial brow saying "Prime Suspect."

I polished off the coffee and a stale roll she had probably been saving for the next war, gave her a brotherly kiss, and headed out into the real world to find out what I could about Prof. Corkney Clatter.

By noon I had learned two important things: He was a noted semanticist and major league literary luminary; and he usually ate lunch at the Oleander Club. I formulated a fictitious but innocent approach to engage this gentleman in conversation, and set out to find him.

As I entered the Oleander lounge I spotted the Prof at a corner table perusing the menu. He was a huge man, jowly and ham-fisted, with a waist circumference at least twice my own. But I had been told that the layers of fat concealed great strength and athletic ability, and his handicap at golf would have been even lower than the very respectable nine he carried, if he could see better over his stomach to line up putts.

Millie was waiting patiently for his order as I neared the table. With a wink at me, the Great One said to the waitress, "I'm in the mood for seafood today; do you have any scruples?"

With barely-concealed disgust, Millie answered, "Yes, and I have qualms, too, but I suggest that you order from the menu." The honors, I think, went to her.

At his invitation I took a seat, and introduced myself as a writer who admired his voluminous literary output and now was in need of his expert guidance. We chatted a bit and quickly established an easy rapport. Of course this process was expedited immensely by my outrageous flattery and his inexhaustible capacity to absorb it. By the time he had polished off his third steak sandwich, and I was nearly through with my tuna-on-white-toast, we were like long-lost brothers, and I decided to move things along.

"Corkney, my writing has gone severely stale; my erstwhile Soaring Similes are mired in the Bogs of Banality. I really need some help on cliches."

"Yes," the Corker replied, "but first let me tell you about our golf match this morning. Waldo and I suckered Shanker and Duff into an even money wager, and we were all set to stick it to them. We weren't going to take any prisoners. . . ."

"Exciting," I offered, "but my problem with cliches—"

"In a minute, boy," Clatter interrupted, "but this story will make your hair curl. We were playing the Azalea course: best ball, match play. We started off slow as molasses in January, but they were hotter than a two-dollar pistol. Even so, I was loose as a goose, but poor Waldo got up tighter than a drum. He was swinging like a rusty gate, and his drives were wild as a March hare. With Shanker's drives and Duff's putting, we were between a rock and a hard place. By the 13th hole, Waldo's face was white as a sheet, and he was shaking like a leaf. We were 4 down with 5 holes to go. Waldo muttered something about our goose being cooked."

"What did you do?" I asked.

"I had a man-to-man talk with him. I told him it wasn't over till the fat lady sang. Just to relax and play it one shot at a time."

"And that worked?"

"He didn't respond, so I had to take Draconian measures: I asked if he was a man or a mouse. Well, that hit him where he lives. He straightened up stiff as a ramrod, and his eyes bored into me with a stare as cold as a well-digger's navel. On the next tee he really got both cheeks into it and nailed it on the screws. He put some *hurt* on that thing! It took off like a scalded dog and finally landed in position A. From that point on we hammed and egged it. . . ."

"You alternately had good holes?"

"Right as rain. Going into the last hole we were evensteven. I drove first. I climbed all over it and caught it on the sweet spot. It sailed across the dogleg, over the spinach, and finally died in the fairway 125 yards from the green. Waldo yanked his drive OB and was dead as a doornail. Then Duff hit a wormburner into the wet, and it was curtains for him, too. But Shanker got lucky and found the short grass, and it was down to him and me for the

36

whole nine yards. He bounced an ugly iron about 35 feet past the hole. But I chili-dipped, caught it a little fat, landed in the frog hair in front and dribbled onto the smooth."

"You mean you were on the green but a long way from the pin?"

"I was on the dance floor but couldn't hear the band. Shanker was away, but he got the yips and booted it about 6 feet past."

"Then what did you do?"

"I gave him his putt and started to line up my thirty-footer."

"You conceded a 6-foot putt which could tie or win the match?!?"

"Sure as shooting. No guts, no glory. If we go down, we go down in flames. So I stroked that baby real firm RIGHT-HANDED (I'm normally left-handed): never up never in, you know. Naturally it went in for all the marbles. Now what was it it was it you wanted to know about cliches?"

"Well, Corkney, some say that cliches are indispensable to the effective articulation of ideas. . . ."

"That's a crock!" The Corker exploded, "I never use them myself."

"Then your advice is to avoid cliches?"

"Like the plague," The Great One said.

With that, I was able to switch the conversation to Brasher's murder. The Professor's normally benign visage noticeably reddened, and then purpled. He was having difficulty getting his voice to function.

Finally, between clenched teeth he grated out, "that SOB got just what he deserved!" Then after a long pause he added, "Not that I had anything to do with it. But that lowlife was always acting so holier-than-thou, and all the time he was having an affair behind his sweet wife's back. Then, when his wife found out and filed for divorce, he dumped the red-headed Amazon floozie too. Well, at least she didn't let him off easy: it must have been a month before the swelling around his eyes went down after that farewell."

That one descriptive phrase rang my gong. I summoned up enough cool to ask the name of the "red-headed Amazon floozie," but I already knew the answer. Hell, I had cookies and milk with her last night.

I left the Professor digesting his third chocolate eclair, and drove over to the observation tower overlooking the East marsh to do a little heavy agonizing. Just sitting quietly watching a blue heron trying to catch dinner in a nearby lagoon relaxed my nerves enough to get my brain out of panic mode and back into the type of insightful thought that might produce some progress in the murder-solving department. Okay, so I had slept last night with a newly-elected prospect for the title of Murderess of the Month. Actually, this was all to the good. She didn't know what I'd learned from Corkney Clatter, and presumably would welcome me back tonight for light conversation and whatever. Far from shrinking back, I should welcome this opportunity to uncover more evidence. I was a silver-tongued marvel when it came to persuading myself to do something I wanted to do anyway, so it was back to Chez LaMoste.

5.

Next morning I left Dear Dotty's hospitality by first light and headed back to my condo. I was able to raise Billy Bob Tolliver on the phone and report my encounter with Prof. Clatter.

"Good work, Clive. We'll have to keep a close watch on him. Meanwhile, another possible suspect has turned up, and it would be a good idea for you to check him out."

"Sure B.B., who is it?"

"Goes by the name of Kelly Hertz. It seems he's the owner of a local specialty radio shop downtown. It's not the kind of place where you go to buy a $19.95 combination clock-radio-alarm for the side of your bed. They specialize in electronic gear for ham operators and CB's and ship-to-shore and stuff like that."

"What does this have to do with Barry Brasher?"

"Well it seems that Kelly Hertz is quite a guy. He has a large building, and he's made classrooms out of some of the space behind the shop. He recruits volunteers to teach illiterate adults how to read. We've checked it out. It's one hundred percent legit. Hertz doesn't get paid, and his part-time secretary is the only overhead cost."

"Yeah, one of the guys I was talking to at the Oleander Club is a volunteer teacher there. They call it SMILE, which is an acronym for something or other. But I still don't see how Brasher fits in."

"Well, he volunteered to help out as a teacher, and had a run-in with Hertz. Apparently some shouting and arm-waving took place. It doesn't seem in character for Old Barry to volunteer, if you believe most of the testimony we've collected. Maybe you can check it out."

"Shouldn't be any problem. Some Soundingers have signed up as volunteers, and I'll do the same."

I rang off, and put in a call to SMILE.

A pleasant baritone voice answered, assuring me that I had reached SMILE and that I was speaking to Kelly Hertz.

"Mr. Hertz, I'm a new resident of the Soundings and am interested in volunteer teaching. I've heard good things about your operation."

"Thanks, Mr. Trebor, we'd like to have you. Could you come down to the studio for a reading and vocabulary test?"

I hadn't counted on that, but it made sense that you probably ought to be able to read and pronounce at least some of the words if you're going to teach others how to do it. All of a sudden I was as nervous as a border-line sophomore who hadn't studied for the final exam.

Hertz sensed the reason for my hesitation, and laughed reassuringly, "Don't worry, Mr. Trebor, it's natural to be a little concerned about taking a test of any kind. We've had volunteers with graduate degrees in English Literature who almost freaked out just thinking about this little quiz. I'm sure you'll do fine."

With that dubious reassurance, I agreed to stop by the studio in about an hour and hung up. I made myself a steaming brew of Columbia's best mountain-grown in a battered aluminum pot I found in the cupboard next to a cracked china sugar bowl. By the time I'd polished off a cup of this ambrosia, my nerves were settled enough to crank up the Caddy and point her nose toward downtown Savannah.

I parked behind the Radio Shop and entered the back door marked with the single word SMILE. As I entered the door, a big bronzed man of about thirty jumped out of his chair and hurried over to shake my hand.

"I'm Kelly Hertz," he intoned in the friendly voice I recognized from our phone conversation.

I believe strongly in first impressions, and my first impression was that I'd like to have this guy on my side next time the bad guys tried to tie my fragile frame into pretzel-like contours. Heck, I'd like to have him as a friend. His mod haircut and dark shades were not really my style, but on him they looked good.

After a little small talk, Hertz got down to business. "Clive, why don't we get started on the reading and vocabulary test. It's not hard, and my impression from chatting with you is that you'll have no difficulty."

He let me into the next room where a desk was set up with several microphones and control switches, a cassette player-recorder, and a couple of complicated-looking devices I didn't even want to know about.

He turned his face toward me and began to explain what I was to do, at the same time deftly selecting and inserting a cassette in the player. Still looking directly at me, he cued up the tape to the proper beginning spot, and adjusted the sound volume.

"Well Clive, all you have to do is push the 'play' and 'record' buttons to get started, and then push the 'stop' button when you're finished. As soon as Holly gets back from her early lunch, I have to leave the office for a meeting down in one of the bank buildings, so she'll help you fill out a short information sheet for us."

I almost panicked. He was going to leave before I got a chance to find out the first thing about the trouble he had had with Brasher. I had to act fast.

"Gee, Mr. Hertz, I feel a little shaky about this whole thing. One of my friends told me that a guy named Brasher got all fouled up with this test and some sort of confrontation developed. I don't want to get in any trouble just because I screw up the test. I'll do the best I can, but I may not pass."

A thoughtful looked spread over Hertz's tanned face.

"Don't worry about that, Mr. Trebor. There was a problem with that jerk Brasher. Of all the people we've interviewed he was the only one who wasn't a delight to work with. Volunteers aren't paid anything, so they are normally here for altruistic reasons, and only good people do that. But not Mr. Barry Brasher. We found out later that he was trying to make time with one of our young female volunteers. He hoped to be put on her shift as a teaching partner."

"What happened?"

"He did very poorly on the test, and when he came in next day for the results I was going to have to tell him we couldn't use him. As it happened, he got here before I did next morning, and came on to my secretary, Holly Berry. As I entered, I heard her asking him to release her arm because he was hurting her. It takes a lot to get me upset, but that did it. I told him that I was glad he'd flunked the test because we'd never use his services anyway."

"Did he leave quietly?"

"Quite the contrary. He began mocking me, and saying that I couldn't stop him from doing anything he wanted, and made a move toward Holly. Mr. Trebor, I'm not a violent man, but I escorted Brasher out of the office myself. If I ever run across him again I'm not responsible for my actions."

"I don't blame you," I said, but what I was thinking was that we had a new suspect with a strong motive to send Barry to his reward. I also was amazed that Hertz pretended not to know about Brasher's murder.

"Sorry I had to tell you all this unpleasantness, but it has never occurred before, and let's hope it never does again. Go ahead with the test, Clive, and then Holly will help you with the rest. Good Luck." He turned quickly and left me alone in the room with The Test.

My first inclination was to deep-six it, because I'd gotten all I could out of Hertz. But on second thought I might learn something from Holly. Besides, I now viewed it as a challenge, and that always gets my red corpuscles moving. I pushed the appropriate buttons on the cassette machine and began.

The first part of the test was merely to read a couple of selections from a magazine. No problem. Then I began to pronounce each of a list of a hundred words. I was surprised at first at some of the simple words on the list, but upon reflection recognized that I had heard many of them mispronounced frequently in normal conversation. Like 'often,' in which many otherwise literate persons mistakenly pronounce the 't.' A second category which

41

seemed simple at first were local geographical names, but consider that 'Beaufort' in South Carolina is pronounced 'Bew-fort,' while the North Carolina city is pronounced more like 'bo-fort' in a semi-French manner. The third category included familiar foreign names which didn't cause much difficulty. I pushed the 'stop' button with a sigh of relief and headed for the other room to see what I might learn from Holly Berry.

I introduced myself and she reciprocated in a soft voice, then I almost cracked up because it struck me that she really was 'Holly Berry.' What I mean is she was wearing a green suit with just enough of a red blouse showing to simulate a berry in the middle of holly leaves.

She waited for me to get control of myself, then smiled and said, "Thank you, Mr. Trebor, for recognizing my trademark. Anyone as plain-looking as I must find a way to stand out a little bit in a crowd."

It's true she wasn't a raving beauty like Dotty LaMoste, but she sure wasn't ugly, and her smile was bright enough to chalk up quite a few points in my game book. I told her so, and we were friends in no time. As she helped me fill out the form, we started chattering away, and I was able to steer the conversation around to Barry Brasher.

She shuddered. "What a horrible man. I think he might have raped me if Mr. Hertz hadn't come in. I hate to say it, but I'm not sorry he's dead."

So she wasn't pulling the innocent act like Hertz. Very strange.

"Holly, Mr. Hertz gives no indication of knowing that Brasher is dead!"

"I'm sure he doesn't know. He has no TV, and of course he doesn't read the paper. Ironically, the 'text' our volunteers use for teaching is the newspaper, but he's usually too busy to listen to much of that, although we have a monitor right here next to my desk. He's told me to let him know when World War III breaks out, and that'll be sufficient news coverage for him."

"But surely you've told him, after the big fuss he caused you here!"

"But surely I have not. Mr. Trebor, I've never seen him more upset than he was with Brasher, and I don't want to get him in a dither again. Let sleeping dogs lie, I say."

42

That was a cliche worthy of Prof. Corkney Clatter, but it did express her attitude to a Tee, as they say. I bade Ms Berry farewell, and told her I'd phone to find out the results of my test next day.

"We'd much prefer that you come in, if you can. That way Mr. Hertz can go over the test with you, and set up a schedule for you to work."

I agreed. It would give me a second shot at getting information out of Hertz, who had to be somewhere on our list of suspects.

I spent the rest of the day in Savannah at Lieutenant Tolliver's office learning all I could about photography interpretation, and headed back to the Soundings. After a shower and change of clothes at my condo, I headed for the LaMoste diggings, purely to interrogate the suspect, you understand.

Next morning at the breakfast table I gleaned a promising bit of information from the chaff that my nubile friend so generously cast on the wind: if a list was made of all the people who hated Barry Brasher, right near the top would be the monicker of one Winthrop Winchester.

"Yes, Clive, Winnie really hated Barry's guts. They played a lot of tennis together, and although he was a great athlete, Winthrop couldn't beat Barry as consistently as he'd like. When Barry won, he'd make fun of what he called 'Winchester's goofy gamesmanship.' It really ticked Winthrop off. He was so good at everything that I guess he hated to lose to anyone at anything."

"Sounds fascinating. I'm getting into tennis, and I'd be interested to hear what Mr. Winchester has to say," I lied.

Dot made a wry face and replied, "Well don't blame me if he bores you to death. You're probably the only one on the Island who hasn't heard that muscle-bound stiff on his soapbox."

Digesting this morsel along with the last of the Danish, I took a final swig of coffee, gave Dear Dotty a morning-type kiss and set off to confront Mr. Winthrop Winchester.

As hoped, I found my quarry seated in the Tennis Lounge, earnestly conversing with three other men similarly clad in tennis whites. He was a handsome man of about forty, blondish hair, regular features, and bulging muscles filling out his tight cotton tennis shirt. Although he was seated, I wagered that the effect wouldn't be spoiled if he stood up.

Just as I came up, one of the others was saying, "No reason to get upset, Winthrop. Drop the whole thing."

With that, the three of them got up, shook their heads, turned on heel and left the object of their frustration with a fierce scowl on his tanned face. It didn't seem like the best timing for buttering up to Winchester, and I turned to go.

He stopped me. "It appeared that you were looking for me. I'm Winthrop Winchester." He turned on a serviceable smile to replace the scowl.

"Yes, Mr. Winchester, but I didn't mean to interrupt anything," I whimpered in my best subservient manner, and introduced myself.

"No interruption at all," he said pleasantly; "What can I do for you?"

"Well, I'm kind of a beginner at the game, and I've been told that you have some original ideas on improving one's total game," I practically groveled.

At the phrase 'total game' he nodded in satisfaction. "Well Clive, you're on the right track. The game must be taken as a whole, not just as a collection of strokes, which most of these so-called pros do now."

From that point on it was a simple matter for me to engage his total attention by merely looking interested. Once W.W. was assured that he had a fresh audience, he launched into what must have been a well-rehearsed diatribe against teaching methods prevalent in today's tennis culture. The thrust of his argument was that modern tennis pros concentrate only on shotmaking, neglecting the cultural and aesthetic facets so important to devotees of couth, who place appropriate emphasis on style and savoir-faire. He began by discussing the strategy of the serve.

"The biggest problem in serving is to kill time between points while your opponent is stalling or otherwise trying to psych you out. Probably the most common maneuver among unsophisticated players is to bounce the ball on the ground repeatedly with the racquet. It's true that this kills time, but it doesn't exactly build your reputation as a superbly coordinated athlete or even a great

44

thinker. However, a simple variation of this exercise can do just that: bounce the ball with the EDGE of the racquet!"

"But, Winthrop, I have tried this, and sad to say, suffered an embarrassing number of miss-hits."

"Ah, the answer for you, Friend, is to buy one of those new implements with a wide wide frame. All of the major manufacturers have discovered the tremendous demand for more efficient edge-bouncers, and the competition is intense to produce an instrument that works well for the clumsiest of players."

"But I thought those wide frames were designed for superior power in serving or controllability in volleying!"

"That's just a ploy. Nobody wants to admit what they really want the extra width for. It's like a conspiracy of silence between manufacturers and customers."

Winthrop paused to savor the sound of his own articulate exposition. I took the opportunity to up the level of brown-nosing by asking the Sage, "Winthrop, that's good advice for a server; but how about when you're receiving serve?"

"Good question. Most players will crouch alertly with racquet high in front of them, giving every indication of being totally ready for whatever serve comes their way. This is good form, but it doesn't give the server the slightest concern. Although some jocks have been effective with an over-exaggerated show of readiness, crouching low like a Sumo wrestler and swinging the racquet in both hands from side to side, an even more effective approach is to appear to be totally UNREADY. The best example of this in modern times was Michael Chang in the French Open, when, on the verge of exhaustion, he stumbled up to the SERVICE line to receive. Lendl was so confused that he double-faulted for the match. Not many of us have the opportunity for a Coup of that magnitude, but we might do well to emulate a certain lanky old gent here at The Neebrace Racket Club, who awaits service with arms hanging limply at his sides, and a look of bewilderment on his face. Not only does he puzzle the server, but if he gets aced he can convincingly claim he wasn't ready."

Winchester stopped and looked at me like one of the End Men at a minstrel show when the Interlocutor didn't come up with the next question on cue.

I obliged. "Can you give me some pointers on net play?"

"Indeed. All pros teach a netman (or netwoman or netchild) to stand alertly, racquet held at Present-Arms, prepared to hit a return on either forehand or backhand. We can't fault that. But what we're concerned with is the image presented to the enemy by the expression on your face. Unfortunately, what you hope will appear to be a show of intense concentration and aggressiveness, is too often interpreted (correctly) by your opponent as abject terror. This is particularly true if your partner's serve maxes out at 13 miles per hour. In this situation you might try smiling at a private joke, giggling, or even winking at your enemy."

"But what if he winks back?"

"Don't wait around after the set is over."

"Winthrop, you've given me enough to get through a match," I lied, "but I'm often embarrassed by a lopsided defeat, and I don't know what to say."

"Ah, that's the most important lesson of all: what to do after the match is over and you and your partner Fritz Fumberly have lost 6:1 6:1 to a geriatric pair from Hilton Head. Your objective, of course is to convince everyone who watched the debacle that it wasn't your fault. Certainly it won't do to take the noble approach: 'I have no excuses.' They may applaud your honesty but they'll still think you're a lousy player. Or you can take the opposite tack and mumble something about a hairline fracture of the right humerus. That's totally unbelievable, and furthermore you'll be labelled a whiner (and possibly a thumb-sucker)."

Right on cue I piped up, "I don't see any way out of it."

Winchester practically kissed me. "But of course there is a way out. The key to this situation is that it is a partnership game, to be shared 50-50. And since you always take credits for the wins, your partner gets credit for the losses. So your first impulse is to say, 'Fritz's game smells worse than a breeze from the southwest when the bellybutton lint refinery is clearing its stacks.' That won't do at all. Not only will nobody pay any attention, but it rates very low on the Noblesse Oblige scale."

"I can see that won't work, but what will?"

"Glad you asked. Yes, there is an easy way to salvage your tennis reputation and at the same time be applauded for your magnanimity. Consider this approach: 'I surely admire Old Fritz's courage in volunteering to fill in despite his lack of experience.

46

With a little more practice he's going to start getting back some of those shots'. . . . Or this one: 'I don't think Fritz did so badly in view of the terrible ordeal he's been through recently.' This latter one has the additional advantage of making everyone forget the match and start wondering what the hell happened to Fritz."

After W.W. finally wound down, I ordered him another frozen chocolate diet yogurt and steered the conversation toward the late Mr. Brasher's demise. Winthrop, displaying not the slightest soupçon of animosity, intoned that it was such a terrible thing to happen, particularly to one of the real nice guys in the community.

This really pulled my chain. I've seen enough murder suspects play-acting innocence to know how tough it is to pull it off, and here was Winthrop presumably giving an Academy Award performance. Maybe his ridiculous pedantry was a cover for subtle shrewdness. Or maybe Dorothy LaMoste was selling me a large bill of goods. But why would she? And how could she? She hadn't come across to me as a candidate for MENSA, or even as a probable high-school graduate. On my mental list of suspects, W.W. moved down a notch or two, but with puzzling footnotes; and dear Dorothy graduated to the upper quintile.

Time enough to chew this over later, right now I headed downtown to see Kelly Hertz at SMILE. Of course my main objective was to further interrogate him on his connection with Barry Brasher, but I was also curious about the results of my reading and vocabulary test.

As it turned out, I would have to come back another day, because Hertz was not in the office.

"I'm sorry you won't be able to see him," Holly said apologetically, "His back was bothering him this morning, and he had to go to the doctor. He likes to go over the test results with all the applicants, but in your case he said it was OK for me to handle it because you did so well."

She drew a score sheet out of her drawer, showed me the three words I had mispronounced, and pronounced each one in the Webster's approved manner for my edification.

"That's a relief, Holly, I feared the worst. I'm sorry about Mr. Hertz's back problems."

47

"Yes, he's been suffering off and on since that run-in with that horrid Brasher character."

"But he told me he 'escorted' Brasher to the door. Did he mean more than that?"

"I'm afraid so. Brasher swung his fist at Kelly, and got the surprise of his life. The next thing he knew Kelly had twisted his arm behind him and pushed him through the door, out into the hall and launched him like a toy glider into the parking lot."

"What was Brasher's reaction?"

"He screamed a lot of profanity at us, got into his car and left in a cloud of dust. I worried quite a bit about him taking revenge against Mr. Hertz, so when I read about the murder, I was very relieved."

"I don't blame you, Holly, this Brasher doesn't sound like the type you'd want to have gunning for you. But that's all over now."

I thanked Holly for her help, and promised to make an appointment as soon as I could to begin my volunteer duties. All the way back to the Soundings I mulled over what I'd learned about the formidible Mr. Hertz. He surely qualified for our suspect list. Having once suffered from a bad back myself, I can attest that I would consider murdering any rotten SOB who caused it.

6.

I had put aside my thoughts of Kelly Hertz, and was chewing over the discrepancy between what Winchester said his relationship with Brasher was and LaMoste's version of same, as I opened the door of Dorothy's pad and walked right into her waiting arms. The warmth of all that perfect flesh wasn't making it any easier for me to hold onto the idea that this was now the Number One Suspect fondling my bony bod. I managed to break away long enough to regain my sanity, and to perform the practical task of pouring out a dram of Wild Turkey for myself to go with that DuBonnet she already had in hand.

It took all my native cunning to bring the conversation around to Barry Brasher without arousing suspicion.

"Dotty, I've been hearing a lot about Barry Brasher, and you told me about his feelings on the deer situation. You must have known him pretty well."

"Not really all that well, Clive. I'd run into him occasionally around the club, and we had some mutual friends."

"How about his wife? Did you know her pretty well?"

"Gee, Clive, I'm not sure I ever even met her. I heard she was a real good golfer, but I'm just a beginner and never got to play with her," Dorothy answered casually, as if she wasn't too interested in either one of the Brashers, and would like to change the subject.

I persisted. "Didn't I hear that there was a divorce?"

"Yeah, I heard that too. I guess she moved away about the time he was killed," she replied in such a offhanded way that I begin to wonder if this was really my day to get the truth out of anybody.

Nothing I said had any appreciable effect on her composure, except that she wished I would quit all the foolish chatter, because she had a fascinating new exercise she wanted to show me. The glamorous and maybe-not-so-emptyheaded Mme. LaMoste held her position atop the suspect list.

The following morning I did some heavy-duty thinking, and came up with a plan I hoped B.B. would go along with. It involved some travel expense, and he was the Keeper of the Pelf. My phone call got right through, and he agreed to get together with me for lunch at The Greeting Place, an eatery located right here on the Island, but outside the Soundings gates. Tolliver was a sucker for those delicious Kansas City beef sandwiches they served, and they were always willing to add that extra dollop of gravy he craved. Billy Bob was not even close to malnutrition, and he aimed to keep it that way.

After B.B. ravaged the extra large prime rib sandwich, and I came that close to finishing a grilled cheese on white toast, we got down to it. I explained that, although I had obtained a lot of undoubtedly valuable information, and had identified several suspects, I was momentarily stalled. I had a very sturdy hunch that a lot more could be learned from the crime photos, particularly the ones of the bizarre wound on the victim's head. What we needed was an expert in physiology as well as golf equipment, and I knew such a person. I referred of course to Dr. Phineas

Physis, my mentor in the California Desert. Lt. Tolliver didn't seem too impressed with my earnest sales pitch, but to my surprise suggested that I immediately head out there to consult with this wizard. The County would pay for the ticket, tourist class of course.

My first impulse of relief was immediately replaced by one of suspicion—what was the catch; what was his ulterior motive? I didn't have to wait long to hear it. It seems that he had been working on the angle of the Brasher ex-wife, recently divorced with extreme prejudice, lots of acrimony, but zilch alimony. Investigation showed that she had recently left the island and was now in Las Vegas. She was rumored to be making a living, not in a normal job like blackjack dealing or hooking, but as a golf hustler.

My heart skipped 2.3 beats, my eyes dilated, my pulse went ballistic. It couldn't be. Finally I was able to croak out, "What is her name?"

B.B. gave me a long searching look, referred to his notes, and replied, "Fiona."

Then it had to be. How many golf hustlers do you know named Fiona? Hell, how many Fionas do you know period? My lunch companion waited patiently for an explanation he knew was coming. I obliged him.

I told him briefly of meeting Fiona, becoming friends and then lovers, doing the golf gig together. Then, more sadly, I related the innocent little argument that had started when she had proposed that women hit better wedge shots into the green than men. And about how it had somehow escalated as each of us trotted out the petty little grievances that can grow under the pressure of being together 24 hours a day. I told how she had left town without "Goodbye," "Lots of love," or even "Go to hell." That had been three years ago. I finally quit looking for her, and tried to fill the void with copious quantities of Kentucky's finest, but soon found that a few extra whiskies a day don't erase that kind of pain.

B.B. filled me in on what he had learned of Fiona's recent history. She had migrated to Hilton Head where she had done well enough with her own brand of golf instruction at Palmetto Dunes and Hilton Head National and other smooth green pieces of real estate. Apparently she met Brasher at some tournament, and for reasons unknown had married the guy and moved to the Soundings with him. There had been a rocky 18 month marriage, followed by a messy divorce precipitated by Brasher's affair with a local red-head. . . .

"Dorothy LaMoste," I interrupted.

Tolliver gave me a look reserved for those moments when I unexpectedly came up with a piece of information he didn't know I had. Almost an admiring glance, I'd say. Or perhaps more along the lines of 'Even an old blind hog finds an acorn now and then.'

"Yep, Clive, that red-headed Amazon goes by the name of Dorothy LaMoste, and she is one large and sexy woman," he said, and then added with a totally nasty grin, "But I guess you know that."

Uncharacteristically (and wisely) I remained silent.

B.B. continued, "There had been a violent three-way confrontation among Brasher, Mrs. Brasher, and Dorothy, ending with Fiona hating Brasher, Dorothy hating Brasher, and the two women hating each other."

"B.B., I've still got Dorothy LaMoste at the top of my suspect list, but I guess I'll have to add Fiona, although I know she'd have to have plenty of justification to even think of doing such a thing."

"Well Clive, I'll have to take your word as far as what Mrs. Brasher's motives would have to be," B.B. offered, "but I've got to wonder if either one of those women could have struck the blow which deprived society of old Barry. Remember we agreed that it almost had to be a man."

"Yeah, but that was before I'd ever met LaMoste or knew that Fiona might be involved. I've got to point out that Dorothy weighs almost as much as I do, has firm muscles, and is highly coordinated."

Tolliver diplomatically refrained from asking how I knew.

"As far as Fiona is concerned, she hits a golf ball damned near as far as I do, using the same kind of implement that bashed Brasher."

"OK Clive, you seem to know more about these two suspects than I'll ever know."

My point conceded, we planned the next move. I would fly to Palm Springs for my conference with Dr. Physis, then drive a rental car the 250 miles to Las Vegas to find Fiona. After locating her and getting all the information I could, I would fill in B.B. by phone before returning to Savannah.

I phoned Phineas Physis and was immediately rewarded by the sound of his soft cultured voice. He was obviously glad to hear from me, and assured me that it would be a real kick for him to examine the photos and give us the results of his expert analysis. It sounded almost like he would pay us for the privilege, so I didn't bring up the subject of his professional fee. Like Corkney Clatter would say, "Let sleeping dogs lie." Buoyed by this news, I headed for the local travel agency to book a flight to Palm Springs.

As I barged thru the big glass doors of the travel agency, I was greeted by a pleasant young woman with a friendly smile and a name tag saying "Judy," who wanted to know how she could help me. I discarded several clever but inappropriate answers, and said that I wanted to go to Palm Springs by the cheapest way possible. And to show her that she wasn't dealing with a greenhorn, I remarked that I knew the first leg of the trip would be to Atlanta, because even if you die in Savannah you have to go by way of Atlanta to get to heaven. She gallantly suppressed a snide riposte, and proceeded to call up a full TV screen of incomprehensible letters, numbers and symbols. (The Travel Industry generously designs complex computer programs to amaze and delight its appreciative customers). This particular display, she explained, listed all the Savannah-Palm Springs connections in ascending order of price.

"I'll take the first one," I said, "the one that says $149."

"Perhaps," replied Judy, consulting the notes explaining the various subscripts, "but only if you're willing to travel on an odd-numbered Wednesday in Lent."

"Okay, the second one is only $225."

Judy grimaced. "Are you over 65, and will you be accompanied by both of your parents?"

We now moved into the $300 range. "I'll take it," I decided.

Judy smiled. "No problem. But of course there is a 12 hour layover at the International Airport in Grundy Center, Iowa. May I suggest the next one instead. You do change planes at O'Hare Field in Chicago, but it's a good connection."

Now it was my turn to show my stuff. "You blew that one, Lady. My plane arrives at O'Hare at 2:07, and the flight out leaves at 2:17. Even I know that 10 minutes isn't enough between connecting flights!"

"Yes, but an hour and 10 minutes is," she replied without gloating, "since you arrive at Gate K-12, which is on Central Standard Time, and depart from Gate B-11, in the Mountain Time Zone."

I guess I'd forgotten how huge O'Hare is. But it did remind me of the biggest reason the Airlines rely on computers: without them it would be impossible to arrange connecting flights at gates as far apart as possible. And complicating the problem is the necessity of having *all* flights use the gates at the very ends of the concourses. This not only is good walking exercise for the passengers, but it alleviates the airplane parking problem. There are many great airplane flyers, but few good airplane drivers. The airlines once used all gates, but the constant dinging of wings and rudders generated enough aluminum scrap to precipitate a grievance from the Trash Haulers International. Since this Union tends to control the industry, the gates closest to the terminal building were virtually abandoned.

We agreed on a flight leaving Savannah next morning, and Judy accepted my battered American Express plastic in payment. For reasons unknown maybe even to God, the little verifier machine on her desk whipped that card right on through, without even pausing in astonishment at the plethora of little credit difficulties it bore witness to. I have a theory that those machines aren't really connected to anything, because no one of my acquaintance has ever witnessed a card being rejected, no matter how shaky the credit rating.

I headed on back to the LaMoste version of heaven-on-earth, and again allowed myself to be led to the love seat.

"I'll fix a bourbon for you while you tell me about your day, dear Clive," my close personal friend intoned.

"Just some business downtown," I lied. "But I did talk to a former client out in Palm Springs, and we're close to a settlement on what he owes me. I'm flying out there tomorrow to get everything signed, sealed and delivered. May take a few days."

Dorothy's mobile features registered despair at the thought of being deprived of my company. She handed me my drink and sat very near to me. If I didn't know better I'd have sworn I heard a small sob escape her lips.

"There's a lot of sadness in this world," I murmured, holding her close, "and we'll just have to get through our share of it as best we can."

Naturally that cheered her up no end, and we began to talk about this and that, each of us trying without much success to find out more about the other. After awhile Dot fetched from the kitchen a Caesar's Salad she had crafted with her own two hands, and again sat very close to me. This time while she nibbled my earlobes I nibbled on the salad, an altogether more sensible reaction than I had exhibited at the first confrontation with earlobe nibbling.

When the salad was finished I allowed myself to be dragged kicking and screaming to the fun-and-games area of the apartment. There, I'm ashamed to say, while Ms. LaMoste was having her way with me, my emotions were dragging me this way and that, with thoughts of Fiona and the old days all mixed up with the here and now which was Dorothy. It didn't help a whole hell of a lot that both of these desirable women were pretty high on anybody's list of murder suspects. Dear Dotty didn't seem to notice my state of mind, and joyously set about to make me as happy as a man can be under those circumstances.

She soon drifted off into the sleep of the innocent, but I wasn't so successful. Finally I sunk into a restless semiconsciousness troubled by dreams of Fiona and Dorothy wreaking all sorts of indignities upon my scrawny frame, and laughing together as they did it.

Next morning I was glad to have a cup of strong Java and beat a quick retreat in the direction of Savannah International airport, burdened by a lot more than the battered duffle bag in my right hand.

Being a little apprehensive about the whole concept of heavier-than-air flight, I had boned up on the subject, and knew just what danger signs to look for. The first thing I checked on was the aircraft itself. I was looking for one with a high model number like 757 instead a low one like 3, as in DC-3. I also wanted to avoid planes with cute nicknames like Constellation or Stratacruiser or Stuka or Piper Cub. Next I looked for cracked window-glass, large dents in the tail or small flames in the vicinity of the engines. More importantly, I closely studied the crew as they boarded the aircraft. I was ready to leave the plane immediately if the pilot staggered, had a nervous tic, wore cokebottle glasses, or spoke with a Libyan accent. He also lost points if he referred to the various controls as 'do-hickeys' or 'thingamajigs.'

Satisfied so far, I then eyeballed my fellow passengers, looking carefully for certain undesirable types, such as men with dirty beards wearing robes and muttering to themselves; or anyone at all carrying heavy parcels that ticked; or hyperactive young guys in handcuffs accompanied by sleepy old guys with badges and pistols.

Now at last I began to relax, ready to be transported on wings of eagles into the wide blue skies, escaping the bounds of earth and reaching . . . I felt an elbow in my ribs as my three-hundred-pound seatmate tried vainly to achieve a measure of comfort which unfortunate genes, a lifetime of gluttony, and a sixteen inch wide seat were conspiring against. I nodded to him and turned away, but not in time. He now had a captive audience.

"Ain't these little seats the shits?" he inquired.

I had to agree to that.

"I'll tell you what else really burns me," he added, beginning to get into the swing of things, "It's sitting on the ground forever while they dink around for whatever foolish reason. And they tell you it's for maintenance, which is a crock. Happens to me every time."

My porcine pal proved prophetic. Many minutes after scheduled takeoff time, I noticed that nothing at all had happened. Then the static level on the state-of-the-art intercom rose a few decibels, and I strained my ears to decipher AN ANNOUNCEMENT.

My seatmate groaned. "They're going to announce that 'this flight has been canceled for equipment reasons.' The equipment reason they're referring to is that they can't afford to fly *this equipment* with just thirty passengers aboard."

I groaned with him. But what I heard was: 'There will be a slight delay for minor maintenance.'

I fairly cackled in the knowledge that my know-it-all companion didn't know it all. "See, it's not that at all. We're just going to be delayed a few minutes."

"Don't kid yourself, Pal. If we're lucky it's only the Captain going back to the terminal for his tri-focals, and this iron bird will be on its way in twenty minutes. I've got a hunch that today we're not lucky and it's going to be a two-hour wait to install a new Pratt & Whitney."

The fat bastard was right. I started out being amused at the repeated updates, each promising 'only a little bit longer,' but after awhile I wasn't really splitting my sides in mirth at the cabin temperature rising to 99 degrees on the Fahrenheit scale.

At last we were airborne, and it was time for the drinks and appetizers. Not having flown for some time, I was expecting champagne and Macadamia nuts, but these have miraculously changed to Diet Coke and grey peanuts. And speaking of miracles, I always thought the Biblical one of the five loaves and two fishes was great, but that was minor league stuff compared to the way those attendants served an entire planeload with just two cans of cola! (The 4-ounce plastic glasses with 3.8 ounces of ice may have had something to do with it.)

I was still thirsty, and could hardly wait for the coffee; at least they couldn't fill the coffee cup with ice. I confided this to my companion, who by now I knew answered to the name 'Porkly.'

"Yeah, Pal. Now watch this-state-of-the-art airline go into action."

"What do you mean, Porkly?"

"I tell ya, Pal, this outfit has been planning this little maneuver since the day the FAA gave them a license. Watch the organization and timing pay off."

Just as the cabin attendants rolled their square-wheeled carts laden with coffee down the aisles, the signs began to flash: 'Fasten Seat Belts.' Sure enough, we hit enough air turbulence to make coffee-pouring an exercise in agility and daring, exceeded in skill only by the art of coffee-drinking under the same conditions.

"Is that timing or what!" Porkly crowed.

I was impressed. "How do they do it?" I asked.

"It's technology," Porkly explained. "FAA regulations require that coffee be served at the most turbulent parts of the flight, so

56

meteorologists at the headquarters city pore over their isobars and isotherms, and flash the word to the Captain when the bumpiest air impends. He in turn relays the order to the Angels of Mercy who push their carts of lukewarm Java down the aisles."

Somehow, all the coffee got poured and consumed. I felt a whole lot better after having my morning coffee, and was relaxing in my seat when the first signs of Nature's call began to tweak my loins. I unfastened my seat belt and got up to make my pit stop.

"Where do ya think you're going?" my seatmate asked.

I told him.

"Lots of luck, Buck. Do you see those lines of people in the back there? Well they're going to be there quite awhile with only one John in service," Porkly said with perverse satisfaction.

"But there are four Johns back there!" I cried.

"Right, but if you look closely you'll see that three of them have 'Out of Order' signs hanging on the door knobs."

"How did that happen?"

"Didn't I tell you this was a sophisticated airline?" Porkly responded. "The attendants check their watches, and exactly 18 minutes after they serve coffee they hang those signs on the restrooms. It took years of study of Human Physiology, Bladder Control, and General Plumbing Principles to get their timing exactly right."

I still wasn't a great fan of Brother Porkly, but I had to admit he was calling the shots pretty well. At any rate I was salivating at the thought of the next happening, the "airline meal." I should have known that anyone who has had one knows that if God meant us to fly, He wouldn't have made it necessary for us to eat too.

It was breakfast time, but my mentor advised me to ignore the orange juice in the aluminum foil container. "I tell ya, Pal, they had those things tested, and an independent laboratory found that it was physically impossible to open that technological marvel without running up a dry-cleaning bill."

So I went right to the fruit cup of avocado rind and pomegranate seeds. I savored it, because I knew I wasn't going to get this treat in Palm Springs or Las Vegas. Likewise the powdered egg and fried bologna.

I felt lucky that our flight was long enough for them to show an IN-FLIGHT MOVIE. I said as much to my seatmate, who only looked at me in disgust and was soon snoring tunefully in his seat.

Now it isn't true that there is just one movie shown on all airlines throughout the world. That's a vicious, unfounded rumor. In fact, there are *three*. If you're flying to Europe, it's "The Return of the Pink Panther," while Pacific flights enjoy "Crocodile Dundee." Since this was a domestic flight, we got "The Bobbsey Twins at Cloverbank," rated G-Plus. Although those earphones they hand out are ingeniously designed for migraine, that's not a problem after the fourth or fifth flight, because you've memorized the dialogue and can dump the phones. There's nothing more inspiring than a planeload of frequent flyers mouthing the dialogue in unison.

As the sun set in the Golden West, the Iron Bird dipped its wings in salute, and locked onto the approach pattern of the great metropolitan airport below, serving Palm Springs and the Coachella Valley. We bumped to a landing, and I took the Limo to The Old Roadrunner Inn for late dinner and some shuteye. Dr. Phineas Physis would be waiting for me in the morning.

7.

Next morning, after an uninspired breakfast of powdered eggs and Indio Jalapenos unsuccessfully impersonating Huevos Rancheros, I swallowed the last of the lukewarm coffee and escaped this ptomaine palace. I was able to get a cab almost immediately, and headed on out Date Palm Drive to Rte 111. A couple of twists and turns later found me in front of Dr. Phineas Physis' golf villa overlooking the fifth fairway of the Palm Fronds Country Club. My stomach did a half-gainer as I spotted the old Hupmobile in all its black shiny glory sitting regally in the abbreviated driveway. I suffered that excruciating feeling of guilt and repentance that comes from the realization that you've screwed yourself by your own greed.

But yanking my thoughts back to the matter at hand, I walked up through the gate of the neat white picket fence, and activated the head of what had been an old bull's-eye putter, but now served as a door knocker. I waited not more than six seconds for the door to be opened by Phineas himself, his merry grin belying the circumstance that he was in a wheel chair.

"Come in," he said, and his cheery voice meant that he was really glad to see me. Seeing my look of surprise and concern, he waved me impatiently into the adjoining living room and sat me down in an overstuffed chair in the corner, where I could admire the many golf trophies lining three walls.

"Just so we don't waste any time on trivia," he said, "let's dispose of the reason why I'm chained to this albatross on wheels. I moved out here in the desert to let the dry air arrest the onslaught of Emphysema, and it has worked pretty well for the last few years. But recently it decided to reassert itself, and I'm paying my dues for all the Unlucky Strikes and Camel Droppings I put through my chimney for forty years. That quack doctor of mine says that the chances of remission are slight to none. He was a good golfing partner of mine since the Great Depression, but I don't think he ever mastered the arcane art of medicine."

The last was spoken like the proverbial man facing the firing squad, and stalling to light a cigarette in the hope that the cavalry would arrive in time. My heart went out to this gutsy old gent, who seemed more like an old friend than someone I had met so recently.

Then Phineas was all business, demanding to see the photographs, and oohing and aahing as he examined each one. He took out an oversized magnifying glass and zeroed in on the pictures of the fatal wound. After some deliberation, and repeated shuffling back and forth of the different shots, he laid down his glass and rendered judgment.

"This may surprise you," he intoned, "but this poor soul was struck rather severely on the temple with a high-lofted club, somewhere between an 8-iron and sand wedge."

I was a bit surprised, because I had guessed it to be a long iron. It had seemed to me that any full swing with a lofted iron would have imprinted only its bottom edge on the target, because of the angle of the face to the shaft. I expressed this objection to Phineas.

He smiled; "That was my first guess, too," he said, "but careful examination shows otherwise. I can only conclude that the blow was delivered at a rather awkward angle, perhaps necessitated by the close quarters."

Phineas paused as if to convince himself that this was eminently logical, and continued, "And to thicken the plot, I can tell you that the lethal club had square grooves!"

This was a revelation. To a non-golfer or a neophyte the little grooves in the iron clubs all look alike, and may be viewed as a harmless decoration. In fact, it is only to the professional or low-handicap amateur that 'square grooves' are of any consequence.

To start with, grooves are machined into the face of an iron club to impart spin to the ball in flight. This spin causes the ball to fly longer and truer, and to have bite when it hits the green, causing it to check up about where it lands. In traditional manufacture, these grooves have a vee cross-section. Just a few years ago, a creative manufacturer introduced grooves with a square profile. They were touted to be more effective in making a ball check up on the green when hit from the rough or when the grass was wet. There is some evidence that this actually works, but only when struck with the power and technique of an expert. This success caused the ruling bodies of the grand old game to prohibit said square grooves, and precipitated a law suit which still goes on. The relevance for this investigation, though, is that clubs with square grooves are fairly rare, and they are found almost exclusively in the bags of highly proficient golfers. Somewhere along the line that might narrow things down.

I smiled. "Phineas, you may have already earned my airfare; we're grateful."

"I'm happy to be of service. But there are some interesting facets to those excellent photos that I'd like to explore further. I have an old friend who retired from NASA. His specialty was shadow microscopy: analyzing pictures of the moon or Mars, and calculating the elevations of the surface features. I suspect he'll be able to help me out on this, if it's OK."

I readily agreed. Then we went on to look at some of the other photographs. He was particularly interested in the ones of the carpet, showing evidence of some sort of vigorous motion. "There's something about the pattern of these scuffle marks that doesn't seem right to me," he said. "As I try to reconstruct the assault with the golf club, I can't quite visualize how these precise marks were made in this fairly small area. What makes it even more puzzling is how this obviously violent action took place without breaking the large glass case so close at hand. Is it possible that the assault took place elsewhere in the building, and the body was dragged in here?"

"We had the same thought at first," I said. "But there were no signs on the carpet of the body being dragged. Of course it would be possible for a very strong man to carry the late Mr. Brasher and dump him here, but I don't think that would make the kind of marks in the carpet we see in the photos. Furthermore, it wouldn't make the sort of loud noise young Flatbelly heard as he was about the enter the shop."

"I agree with you on all points. I'll have to give this puzzlement a little concentrated mental massage, and see if I can find an explanation for the seemingly inexplicable."

As he said this, I could see the kind of excitement in his sparkling dark eyes that told me I had done the right thing in coming to him for help. He was not likely to give up on this venture until someone stamped 'Solved' on the dossier and filed it away. Again I was pretty sure he would be willing to pay us just to let him work on the case. So, with a slight twinge of guilt, I decided against bringing up the subject of compensating him for his help.

Phineas promised to let me know if he came up with anything in his ruminations about the marks in the carpet, and reiterated his intention to further investigate the photos of the fatal wound with his specialist friend. I thanked him again, and asked him to call a cab for me.

"Not just yet," he said with a twinkle in his eye, "First we have important business to dispose of." With that he wheeled into his kitchen, and shortly returned with a bottle of Fairfax County bourbon and two glasses.

"A toast to the once and future owner of a mint-condition 1940 Hupmobile, custom-made with enough unique features to make it truly one-of-a-kind, a priceless gold nugget in the dross that is today's auto industry. It gives me great pleasure to return it to its rightful owner."

I couldn't believe it. Then as I saw he meant it, I started to choke up, and I might have burst into tears if that had been my style. Dr. P. had just zapped me with a heavy jolt of instant happiness. "You can't do this . . . " I faltered. . . .

"Ah, but I can and will!" he replied. "It was some kind of thrill to be in command of that wonderful machine, and watch the envious eyes of bystanders follow me as I paraded regally by. I'll always be grateful for the short time I had it, but my doctor assures me that I won't be driving anything anymore. I'd been looking for a deserving person to give it to when you called, and who more deserving than you? I saw the terrible sadness in your eyes that day up on the mountain when you gave it to me, and I've felt guilty about it ever since. With one stroke I can assuage my guilt feelings, and at the same time find a happy home for this magnificent machine. Now I don't want to hear another word about it."

It was obvious that he really wanted to do this, so who was I to thwart an old man's wishes? We toasted each other and the Hup, he gave me the title and the keys and practically pushed me out the door. As I got in and caressed that soft maroon leather seat, I could only think of one thing: Will I wow them in Las Vegas tonight!

Before heading out of town I had a mission to accomplish. I stopped in the three best wet-goods emporiums in Palm Springs, and bought out probably the city's entire supply (4 bottles) of Rip Van Winkle Bottled-in-Bond 107 proof. I hailed a cab and had him deliver my package to a golf villa on the fifth fairway of Palm Fronds Country Club. Anybody who liked Fairfax County would go ape over Rip Van Winkle.

All the way up the valley past those ten thousand windmills and through the pass on down the long slope to San Bernardino, I just sat in a daze and let that beautiful car drive me. I joined the real world long enough to hang a right onto Interstate 15 and accelerated up the canyon to the high desert. Ahead of me lay about three hours of the most nothing driving in North America, but the Hup smoothed out the heat ridges and settle bumps of the aging pavement, and nearly mesmerized me with the muted rumble of its powerful engine. The bitter-sweet disconnected thoughts of Fiona and me inhabited my brain until the flashing neons in the distance alerted me to my approach to Sin City, Gommorah on the High Plain.

According to B.B.'s information, I'd probably find Fiona at the Calloused Concubine, one of the newer posh resorts on the Strip. It sported a first rate golf course along with a luxury hotel and large casino. I checked in at the Riviera down the Strip, an old stomping ground where I'd feel a little more secure in the tense time ahead. I carefully stashed the Hupmobile in the parking garage, because there were always cabs waiting to take you anywhere on the Strip you didn't feel like walking to. After tidying up minimally in my room, I went downstairs to carry out my patented routine for winding down in Las Vegas.

Step one was to sit at one of the cheap blackjack tables, play conservatively, and order free bourbons from the shapely House drink-pushers. Of course the House does not pour free drinks so generously through benevolence or altruism; many years of experience have taught that a well-lubricated tourist can lose faster than a tee-totaller. But in my modest way, I took just a wee bit of advantage of mine hosts. By minimum betting, and not hitting 13 or 14 when the dealer is showing a bad card, I could come close to breaking even while downing maybe two quality bourbons.

Then I'd move to step 2, which meant deserting the gaming table for the in-house restaurant where I could get an excellent chicken sandwich (hold the mayo), and play a one dollar lotto card thoughtfully placed next to the napkin holder for my convenience. I'd wash it (the sandwich, not the card) down with a steaming black coffee before graduating to Step 3 back up in the privacy of my room.

This entailed a warm jacuzzi, and a bourbon on extremely cold rocks, before melting between the sheets for a dreamless sleep. This was my version of the old Scandinavian routine of a steaming sauna, followed by a little self-flagellation with birch branches, culminating in a dive into an ice-bound fjord. I've always thought my method to be clearly superior, and it nearly always worked, but tonight my mind wouldn't let my tired old body relax. Seemed like my mental birch branches were doing a pretty effective flagellation routine on my already-battered psyche.

8.

Next morning I was up not-so-bright, but somewhat early by Las Vegas standards. My enthusiasm for the task at hand hadn't been improved a whole lot by a meager three hours of uneasy sleep, and the persistent flashbacks to the Happy Times with Fiona.

The human brain apparently is made up of two halves, one of which is a whiz at logical thinking and all that sensible stuff, while the other shines when it comes to emotions and impulses and other functions not too likely to help you make a living in a hard world. I once read of an experiment on the brain of a monkey in which a structure called the Corpus Callosum, connecting the two halves of the brain, was severed. This was expected to eliminate coordination between the two halves. An unexpected result was that that ape was able to learn two separate tasks in the time required for an ordinary animal to learn one. I was beginning to wonder if somehow someone had severed my Corpus Callosum, because the two halves of my brain weren't coordinating too well, though each was performing the type of assignment it was supposed to. One side was sure churning up a storm of heavy duty emotions, while the other side was going about the business of finding Fiona to question her as a suspect in a brutal murder.

Bolstered by several cups of Java and a half-finished bagel without lox, I set forth afoot down the Strip to the Calloused Concubine. It was one of those clear cool delightful sunny days that Las Vegas can lay on you now and then, and in normal times I would enjoy the walk past all the garish hostelries and Palaces of Chance, watching the faces of the all-night gamblers as they emerged, delighting in the smiles of the winners, and empathizing with the losers. Whoever first wrote about the agony of defeat probably was in Vegas at the time, because my rough scoring this morning showed the loser: winner ratio at about ten to one.

It brought to mind an old friend of mine, a compulsive gambler, whose otherwise happy marriage was driven onto the rocks by his alarming tendency to roll snake-eyes with his last several big ones piled on the craps table. Before the breakup, a well-meaning friend had written a bit of doggerel for a birthday party for the gambler's wife:

"Don't let him go to Vegas,"
A tearful helpmate said,
"Before he goes to Vegas
I would rather see him dead."

"For if he goes a-gambling,
He'll surely lose his poke,
And come back from Nevada
Dead sober and stone broke."

"We're told to leave our footprints
Upon the sands of time,
But I will put MY footprints
On that S.O.B.'s behind."

That little goodie from Erato's bag brought a lot of chuckles from the literature lovers assembled, but apparently inspired Wifey to put her figurative footprints on Hubby's figurative behind, by means of the filing of official divorce papers.

Remembering all this did nothing at all to lighten the emotional load I was staggering under this morning, but by then I was in front of the Calloused Concubine and had little choice but to go in. After a futile survey of the eating areas and the casino, I headed down a corridor which I knew from experience led to the Pro shop and links. I had run into the current pro, Big John Hurt, a few times, and was on speaking terms with him. My luck was good, and I found him in the shop, his usually dour expression supplanted by a reasonably serviceable smile.

"Hi ho, Clive-erino," spake John, and I immediately began to wonder what the SOB wanted from me. He hadn't been all that warm to me two years ago when I had sunk that 18-footer to clean out his total supply of petty cash. But further conversation revealed that John had forsaken gambling for religion, and one of the tenets of his sect was to be a friend to man, no matter the past unpleasantnesses. Seemed like a good opportunity to get a lead on Fiona's whereabouts, if Big J had any clue.

"John," said I, "It is splendid to see you again, and you'll be happy to learn that I too have seen the error of my ways. But I come looking for a dear friend, one who may not yet have seen the light of virtue. I refer to the fair damsel Fiona Brasher, or maybe Fiona Feather, if she's back to the name she was born with."

Hurt let out a long whistle. "Fiona Feather it is, and she has indeed been here. Never saw a golfer, man or woman, with as smooth a swing. And a real looker, too. When that woman smiled, she could charm the dead back to life, and believe me she did the same to a lot of golfers around here who weren't quite dead. You damn bet I know Fiona."

Trying mightily to control my patience, I asked, "Have you seen her recently, and do you know where I could find her?"

"Answer is No to both your questions. She had been spending a lot of time here, befriending lonely tourists who preferred losing on the links to doing same much faster at the tables inside. I had no objections. They were going to lose anyway, and at least this way they got some fresh air and exercise and companionship. I'm confident she didn't cheat anybody, she just seemed to raise the level of her game when the chips were down; what we call a money player, like Trevino or Ballesteros. Most of them didn't seem upset if they lost. But apparently, one of the Hotel owners' kin was among the sheared lambs, and mentioned it to his relative in passing. I got the word toute suite and passed it on to Fiona. That was three weeks ago and I haven't seen her since. I have a hunch she might be at the Cactus Canyon."

I thanked John profusely, purchased one of his overpriced genuine ersatz imitation synthetic leather all-weather golf gloves to show my appreciation, and vacated the premises.

I wasn't too optimistic about my chances of finding Fiona doing business at the Cactus Canyon, because the last I heard the management there took a very dim view of any sort of serious wagering other than at the tables. She would have to be very cagey indeed to make any serious inroads into the pocketbooks of the patrons of that worthy establishment. Nevertheless, it was the only lead I had, so I soon found myself in the Cactus Canyon pro shop, desperately trying to recognize someone I knew who might give a helping hand. This proved futile, so I was forced to play the hand that was dealt me, and engaged the young assistant pro behind the desk in friendly conversation. That kid was well trained; he was all "Yessir" and "Nosir" and "I don't know sir" but he obviously wasn't going to tell me anything about anybody. I finally gave up and went back into the hotel to try Plan B.

I seated myself at one of the Cactus Canyon bars, trying to get the lay of the land. Knowing Fiona's fondness for Stingers-on-the-Rocks, I discreetly questioned the bartender as I nursed a short Wild Turkey straight. No, he hadn't run into any lovely female ordering that particular drink or he sure would have remembered. I got the same answer from several waitresses who were being very hospitable to me as I moved from one blackjack table to another, ordering as few bourbons as I could and still keep the conversation lines open.

The life of a private eye is not an easy one, and I was about to toss in the towel for the day, when the bartender I had become friendly with motioned me over. I was there in a couple of microseconds. He introduced me to the guy who was relieving him for the evening, one Frank Fitzwater. Frank thought he might have seen the woman I had described, and the Stinger-on-the Rocks routine seemed familiar too.

Frank rolled his eyes and whistled softly in tribute to the picture that had just been projected on the screen of his modest brain.

"Yeah Buddy, this broad I'm thinking of may be the one you're looking for. Did she have long shiny coal-black hair?"

I ignored the vulgar synonym for 'lady,' and affirmed that he had accurately described Fiona's crowning glory.

"And did she have the biggest soft brown eyes along with an OK face and a knockout figure?"

"That's her!" I exclaimed, (although if I hadn't been so excited I would have said 'that's she'). "Have you seen her recently?"

"Well, she has come in a few times about ten or eleven in the evening. She was something special. Real quiet and polite and friendly, and when she smiled it just made you feel good; know what I mean?"

"Frank, I know exactly what you mean, but have you seen her recently?" It was all I could do to keep from grabbing him by the throat and squeezing out an answer to my question.

"I haven't seen her in the last ten days, that's for sure."

I groaned to despair. So near and yet so far! Would I ever catch up with her?

"Hey old Buddy, don't give up so easy; the reason I haven't seen her recently is I've been on vacation. Up till then she was in here about every other night for awhile. I bet she'll be in tonight or tomorrow night, what you want to bet?"

I wasn't going to bet. If my Old Buddy Frank said it, it had to be true. Cling to that thought.

For the day-bartender's thoughtfulness, I slipped him a green one which he stuffed into his pocket as he headed for the exit without even checking to look at the denomination. I suffered a pang of regret that I had given him a twenty when a five would have sufficed, then turned my attention to befriending Frank Fitzwater. In a manner of minutes, we were really Old Buddies, and I told my Old Buddy that I would return by ten o'clock. He promised to keep his eyes open.

Back at the Riviera, I lowered my tired old bod into the steaming Jacuzzi, and made an attempt to plan what I would say to Fiona when I found her. Maybe the steam was leaching out too many alcohol fumes via my brain, because I wasn't able to come up with an approach which made my sense whatsoever. "It's good to see you, you're a suspect in a brutal murder, come back to Savannah with me to confess" didn't quite handle it. I arrived at the only solution any brilliant, thoughtful, sane man would: I would play it by ear.

About nine-fifteen, freshly shaven and conservatively clad in navy blue blazer with royal blue slacks and light blue checked sports shirt, I headed out on foot for the Cactus Canyon. Fiona had always liked me in blue, and if tonight was to be the night, at least I would make the right sartorial impression. I was nearly to my destination when I heard a car approaching at high speed from the rear. Some protective sense told me there was something terribly wrong. I turned to see a large black sedan hurdle the curb and head down the sidewalk directly at me. In the small fraction of a second's grace that my premonition had afforded I leapt into the bordering Rosemary bushes, falling hard on my shoulder among the spiked branches as the dark menace roared by. I was back on my feet quick enough to see it hit somebody or something a little further down the sidewalk, before careening out into the street and disappearing in the distance. As I headed up the walk I could see a crowd gathering about 200 feet away, and deduced that the runaway vehicle must have struck a person before returning to the roadway.

Nobody seemed to be doing anything except staring, and since I was well trained in first aid and other emergency procedures, I pushed through the ring of onlookers to see if I could be of assistance. The victim was a young woman, whose long black hair cascaded across a beautiful gold lame' gown sheathing her shapely torso. I gently turned her face up to see if she was conscious, and Armageddon loomed. It was Fiona.

Sitting in the hospital waiting room, my thoughts were going in nineteen directions at once. Somebody on the scene of the accident had been alert enough to dial 911 while I was bending over Fiona, trying to will her back to consciousness. There were no visible marks on her, and she was breathing, but gave no other sign that she was occupying the world of the living. The ambulance had gotten there in less than three minutes, and being the only person at the scene who knew her I was allowed to go with her in the ambulance to the hospital. Now I was just a concerned bystander with nothing to do but let my imagination torture me.

Of course my main concern was for Fiona's recovery, but several extraneous thoughts began to intrude. Something in my brain kept nagging at me, and suddenly I knew what it was. As I had thrown my fragile frame into the Rosemary bushes to escape vehicular assault, I hadn't had time to identify the model and make of the car, only observing that it was a big black sedan, but I had seen something else. The license plate bore the image of a large peach on a garish orange and white background. It could only be from Georgia, and all you geography buffs will recognize that the fair city of Savannah is indeed in Georgia.

Although several witnesses to the accident had opined that the driver of the car was under the influence, citing its erratic progress, I hadn't been so sure. Now that I knew it was a Georgia car, I had to consider that the driver could be someone from Savannah who didn't like what I might have learned in the investigation of the murder of one Barry Brasher. Of course I had to consider also that it might have been Fiona they were after, but I pretty well discounted that because the car had leapt the curb and come right at me, and had only encountered Fiona a couple hundred feet further along. In either case, it wasn't going to help me get to sleep that night.

About that time the young resident who had taken charge when Fiona was brought in, entered the waiting room and headed right for me. I sagged visibly in relief when I saw the broad smile on his face.

"Mr. Trebor, our friend is alive and in about as good condition as we could hope for. It appears that she suffered only a . . ." and I tuned out my hearing to concentrate all my energy on holding the thought that Fiona was OK.

The young doctor concluded his evaluation of the patient with a few more technical terms that proved to us and to himself that he indeed was a real doctor, adding almost as an afterthought that her only problem seemed to be a concussion. Presumably she would be held overnight for observation, and then would be free to go.

A frown then crossed the handsome face of our aspiring Albert Schweitzer, and he blurted out, "This is rather strange, Mr. Trebor, but when she asked if anyone had come to the hospital with her, we naturally gave your name. Her reaction was extraordinary: she seemed puzzled in the extreme, and kept protesting that it was not possible. . . ."

"Don't worry about it, Doctor, it's a little complicated. Did she want to see me?"

"Indeed she did, and she's waiting for you right now. You may go in."

Elation was fighting a pretty good battle with Apprehension as I went down the hall to Fiona's room. Did she want to see me for my own sterling self, or was she just curious about how I happened to be there?

I got a pretty good idea as I went into her room. The lovely smile that always made her beautiful face even more striking lit up that drab little hospital cell, and carried me along for the ride.

"Fiona," I intoned with a show of originality.

"Trebor," she replied. That was a good sign, because she never called me that when she was peeved with me.

We seemed to be at impasse, so I called upon my massive talent for Glib to get things going. "Fiona, you can't believe how great it is to see you again, even in bed . . .," and then I realized how that had sounded and tried to rescue myself by adding, "I mean a hospital bed . . ." shoving my moccasin further down my maw. But when Glib craps out, sometimes Stumble comes to the rescue.

Fiona broke into her patented musical laugh that always seemed too big for her. "Clive, you're much too much, and I love you for it . . ." and she realized that she was too close to committing to something she wasn't ready for.

Always the gentleman, I came to the rescue by laughing with her, and the sudden tension evaporated. She immediately started interrogating me as to what in the liquid hell I was doing in Las Vegas and was I looking for her and why.

I had been preparing for that sort of questioning as I cooled my heels in the waiting room, and had decided to play it cozy. The trick was to delay direct answers without actually lying. I wanted a little time to re-establish a relationship before getting into the down and dirty of the murder and her possible connection to it.

It seemed like a good strategy, and it took Fiona nearly 30 seconds to significantly damage it. She had always been able to cow me when it came to verbal maneuvering, and apparently had lost none of her virtuosity in the few years since we parted ways. I found myself telling her most of the story, leaving out certain insignificant details—like Dorothy LaMoste. Then I waited for her reaction, possibly violent, because after all I was delivering the message that someone in authority might be considering pinning Murder-One on her, and I was at least convinced enough of the plausibility of it to deliver the black spot.

I braced for an explosion that never came. I looked for Surprise and Fury and Hurt and a few of their siblings, and all turned up missing. Instead, she gave me a long contemplative look and began to speak in the low steady tone of someone who is facing up to something she knew had been coming.

"Clive, I knew about Barry's death: I was in Savannah when it happened, cleaning up a few of the details of the wreckage of our marriage. I wasn't after his money or anything he owned, but that SOB was trying to take some of the material goods I had brought into our holy union and I wasn't about to let him get away with it. I didn't quite get it all settled before some noble soul did the deed for which I'd like to award a gold star. And imagine, he did it with a seven iron or such! I got a few chuckles when I heard that."

She finished off this little speech with an attempt at a smile, which immediately degraded to a trembling lip, closely followed by a sob and enough tears to dissolve any thoughts I might have had about grilling her on her part in the murder. Some things have to wait for the proper time and place, and this was one of those things. I held her for a long time, and just as I was working up to give her some competition in the weeping department, she pulled away from me, gave a dampish smile, and said, "Clive, I'm so glad you're the one they sent. I'd hate to have to cry on your friend B.B.'s shoulder."

With that we steered things around to where she was staying (The Riviera!), and the details of checking her out of the hospital. Just then the resident Florence Nightingale marched in, fixed me with a high-test glare and informed me that THE PATIENT needed to sleep, that she was there with a pill to assist same, and that I was to crawl back into whatever hole I had come from until tomorrow. I can take a subtle hint as well as the next one, so I eased out the door with a parting promise to Fiona that I would be back in the morning to check her out of the loving care of this establishment.

Surprisingly, I was able to sleep a few hours after all. I guess it was the release of tension in finding Fiona, and her obvious pleasure in seeing me, that did the trick. At any rate, I was back at the hospital bright and early, and had to go through only four vending-machine coffees before she was released from the angels of mercy and entrusted to the responsible care of one Clive Trebor, the guy with the happy smile and the very sore shoulder. (Rosemary bushes are not to be confused with feather beds.)

Over my objections and against the strict instructions of Young Dr. Kildare, Fiona insisted that we walk back to the Riviera. Something about stretching her legs and breathing the fresh air. But I could be adamant too, and she agreed to take a cab as far as the Cactus Canyon, which seemed to be her real objective anyway. About a hundred yards short of the hotel I told the cabbie to let us out. He obviously hadn't learned his trade in New York, because he had smiled at us when we got in, and had refrained from verbal misanthropy the whole trip, thus earning an oversize tip from Congenial Clive the workingman's friend.

We started walking down the sidewalk toward the spot where the Rosemary bushes saved me the night before. "Right there's where I jumped into those vegetative man-eaters. I never knew a bush could have so many little built-in daggers. If my wounds ever heal, I'll still smell like that damned wild condiment till the day I die. The undertaker won't have to embalm me, I'll be preserved in Rosemary."

"Clive, don't talk about dying," she said with a shudder, "and don't bad-mouth the friendly flora that saved your life."

"A thousand apologies to you and Rosemary. But to get serious, I think that driver was after me, and it's totally unlikely that he had you in his sights."

"Why do you say that?"

"Well, if he was after you, the driver wouldn't have mounted the sidewalk so far ahead of where you were."

Fiona began to study the sidewalk and gutter and curb.

"Clive, here are the tire marks where the vehicle leaped the curb. Now sight down the line to where I was struck."

I saw what she meant. "Another theory from Uncle Clive shot in the butt," I admitted.

At the point where we were standing, the curb was no more than four inches high, but it immediately began tapering higher and reached an imposing 12 inches a short distance beyond where I had been walking. To get to either Fiona or me the car would have had to hop the low curb at just the spot he actually did. And, ominously, the driver probably had worked this out earlier, meaning that he or she had either followed one of us, or in the case of Fiona, had become familiar with her routine.

"Yes, Clive, he could have been after either one of us, but I think he was after me."

We set off toward the spot where she had flirted with the Grim Reaper the night before. The only clue that anything at all unusual had happéned here was a set of tire tracks slanting across the curb as the car had left the sidewalk and returned to the street.

"Look at this, Clive," she said quietly.

73

I saw, but couldn't immediately tell what she was driving at. I said as much.

"Clive, there are no tire marks on the sidewalk."

By now I realized that I was missing something that any moron would catch on to, but I just motioned for Fiona to go on.

"Brake marks, Clive, there are no brake marks. That SOB should have at least tried to brake the car before he hit me." After a pause she added, "Unless he wanted to hit me."

That put a whole new coat of paint on this unpretty little picture we were trying to reconstruct. But no use trying to allay Fiona's apprehensions with explanations; hell, she was a step or two ahead of me on this thing already. Better to find out if she had any reasons to suspect that someone was after her with malice aforethought.

"Fiona, is there any reason anybody in Vegas might be after you, maybe a lamb you might have shorn on the links or a jilted lover?" I winced at the last phrase, and Fiona laughed at my discomfort.

"Very smooth, Cliv-o, you always had a way with words when you were jealous." Then she turned serious. "There has been no one in the love-and-kisses department since I left dear dear Barry. As for the links pigeons, I've managed to leave them all smiling, happy to have gotten so cheap a lesson from such a charming teacher." She grinned at the last adjective to show that she was merely quoting someone else.

I hesitated a few seconds to mull it over and then came out with it. "Fiona, the car that hit you had Georgia plates." I watched her reaction, but couldn't read anything except that she was considering the implications.

Finally she said, "there are only two people in Savannah who might have really hated me, and ex-hubby is history. That leaves one Dorothy LaMoste, the bitch who had the hots for Barry. Except that if she had run me over it would have been on a broom."

I was shocked at the stream of pure venom coming from the normally kind and charitable woman I loved, and at the same time I was almost panicking at the thought that when we got back to Savannah she'd surely find out about LaMoste and me. It didn't take a lot of contemplation to decide to let that sleeping dog lie until I could figure out a way to keep him from biting.

About then Fiona looked much too pale and drawn to suit my taste, so I called a cab that happened by and we rode on over to the Riviera. I was pleased to see that she had a very comfortable two room suite, and it had a settled look as if she had been there quite a while. She confirmed this.

"I didn't know how long I was going to be staying in Vegas, so I didn't want to rent an apartment, and I hate a crowded little room, so I was lucky to find this place. I'm not tied down with a lease, and I can well afford it. Turns out that there was some money left in the family and I inherited my share. That's why Barry wanted to marry me: he would do anything for money."

All this came out in one breath, as if she was apologizing for something. I wanted to say that I would marry her with or without the money, but this wasn't the time for it. She was obviously exhausted, so I turned down her bed for her, gave her a platonic kiss and instructed her to call me at my room as soon as she finished her nap. Then I did the last thing in the world I wanted to do: I left.

I went down to the coffee shop for a tuna on toasted white and an orange juice, lost ten bucks in the slots, and hurried on back up to my room. I wanted to be there when Fiona called. Sitting around gave me a chance to assess where we were on the case. Fiona hadn't said anything to make me a lot more suspicious of her. Sure, she hated Barry B., and Dorothy LaMoste, but we already knew that. And she admitted to being in Savannah when Brasher was killed, but that didn't prove anything. The one thing that did spark my interest was her remark that it was fitting that Brasher was killed with 'a seven iron or such.' How could she know that if only the police and myself and Dr. Physis were supposed to be privy to it? But when you look at all the people in the police lab and administration and criminal investigation who knew it, it wasn't too unusual that it leaked out. It would take a helluva lot more than these trivial little observations to make me believe that Fiona could commit murder.

About the time I had arrived at this point, the phone rang. It wasn't Fiona, but Phineas Physis. He had his informal network of mavens working on the case, but was just reporting that they hadn't quite resolved one very interesting hypothesis of his. This was just a progress report, and he would get back to me. No, at this time he didn't have any details on this hypothesis, but would let me know when the time came. I was beginning to feel like I was adrift in a sea of enigmas without so much as a paddle, or even a first class clue.

The second time Ma Bell paged me I was on that phone in half a nonce, willing it to be Fiona. It was. She was feeling much better, and would I care to mosey down to her apartment to discuss the evening's program? I would.

It was already six o'clock, so I shrugged into my best blue blazer and headed for suite 777. The radiant lady who came to the door bore no resemblance to the bedraggled waif I had left here just hours before. The pasty complexion had been replaced by the glowing tan I always associated with her, and her understated makeup accented rather than overcame the beautiful eyes and flawless features. But best of all, the smile was there. No one smiled like Fiona.

"You're looking great," I understated.

"Nice of you to notice, kind sir."

And we went on from there. She had been busy before she called me, ordering from room service a bottle of Wild Turkey for me, Tanqueray for herself and assorted hors d'oeuvres to be washed down. We began to fill in the gaps of our three year separation for each other.

"Clive, after that silly argument and our breakup, I didn't knew what I wanted to do, but I had to get away. I spent a few weeks at the old hotel at Pinehurst, got into a few games with the tourists who had come for the five golf courses, and made enough scratch to head on down to Sea Island. Lovely spot, the Cloister. Lots of easy money, too. Then I got the itch to move again, and this time it was Colorado Springs. It was like I was running away from something, rather than going toward something I wanted to find. At the Broadmoor I was thrilled with the beauty of the mountains and the lush green of the manicured fairways, and thought I might just settle down there, but after awhile I got the urge again, and I was off for Hilton Head where I had friends to stay with. That's where the old family lawyer tracked me down to let me know that everyone had died off and I was inheriting enough to live comfortably for the rest of my days. And Barry Brasher smelled money like you and I smell a good steak on an outdoor bar-be-cue. I met him at one of the clubs. The guy had a smooth swing, and an even smoother line of chatter. Looking back, it's hard to believe that I could have gone for that phoney, but I guess I was getting desperate for some stability, and Barry seemed to offer it. He took me to Slipaway Slough, and I just loved it. The quiet paths through the trees, the six fabulous golf courses, sunset on the marsh, the way the homes blended in with nature . . . it was all there. Of course what I didn't know was that friend Brasher was overdue on his mortgages, his credit cards, and also to a couple of loan sharks who were starting to get very impatient with him. All I was to him was a real bargain in refinancing: nothing down and nothing a month."

She paused and waited for me to reciprocate. I told her as much as I could about what had happened to my life in the last three years, omitting only a few little indiscretions, and one king-sized indiscretion known as Dorothy LaMoste. I'd still have to face that one before we got to Savannah.

I wound up the Adventures of Super-Clive, and asked Fiona where she'd like to have dinner.

"Would it be OK if we stayed here? I don't really feel up to dressing for a nice restaurant, and I'm not hungry for hamburgers."

"Your wish is my command," I intoned grandly, pleased that I would have her all to myself for an hour or two.

"We can call room service for dinner, or we could subsist on these hors d'oeuvres. We seem to have more than I anticipated."

"More than we can ever finish," I agreed, pouring a modest dollop of Wild Turkey in my glass. "Also, this will give us a chance to go over plans for the trip back to Savannah."

"Well, to start with, Clive, I have nothing holding me here in Nevada. I was thinking of moving on anyway, when you showed up."

"How do you feel about going back to Savannah?" I asked.

"In a way I look forward to it with pleasure, because I'd gotten to love the beauty and peace of The Soundings. But overriding that, I dread it because of what happened there, and the fact that I'm a natural suspect in it. I've known all along though, that I'd have to go back and face it. And now is certainly the time, having you to stand up for me through the rough spots." She smiled wanly.

Nothing could be truer. I was committed to this lady for life, and wasn't about to let the system grind her up. Anyway, suppose she WAS the one who polished off old Brasher; she had a damn good reason. But I'd better stop thinking like that: of course she was innocent, and it was up to one C. Trebor to prove it.

We decided to spend a couple more days in Las Vegas, play a round of recreational golf, and then head east in the Hup.

Having decided our future beginning *tomorrow,* how about *to-night?* I desperately wanted to stay right where we were, but would have to let Fiona decide. She sensed what was running though my mind, and was very gentle with me.

"Clive dearest, part of me wants very passionately to have you stay here with me, but I need a little more time to get everything straight in my mind. It has been three years you know, and the last twenty-four hours haven't been exactly ho-hum. Let's just say goodnight at the door and see what develops tomorrow."

What could I do? What I did was take a long Jacuzzi in my room followed by a bourbon and a lonely bed.

9.

Next morning Fiona called before I'd finished shaving. "Clive, I've been out walking, and it's such a beautiful day. Let's go on a picnic."

"Whatever you say, kid."

What I was thinking to myself was 'for God's sake, woman, how about letting an old fart with a sore shoulder have a little coffee to get his heart started first?'

We met down in the coffee shop, had a little coffee, a little breakfast, and a lot of pleasant chatter. Then we arranged with the kitchen to pack us up a nice lunch to go with the bottle of Chardonnay she had in her mini-fridge. While Fiona gathered all this stuff up, I unpawned the Hup from the garage, and we took off for Hoover Dam and Lake Meade. It's a short drive. We duti-fully did the tourist thing, taking pictures all over the dam as if we'd never seen it before, and visiting the overlooks to view the broad expanse of lake dotted with so many small boats.

Then after a few false starts, we found the winding road that led us to the quiet little spot where we'd picniced once in the good old days. Surprisingly it hadn't changed much, the weather was delightful, the chicken sandwiches delicious, and the Chardonnay even better. Just like on daytime TV, life can be beautiful. Fiona and I were becoming reacquainted in a leisurely unforced way that promised to develop into something durable and satisfying and right.

As often happens when the sun shines so brightly and the birds sing so sweetly, a little gray cloud crept across our horizon. Well, it wasn't little and it wasn't gray and it wasn't a real cloud. What it was, was a black Lincoln town car with dark tinted windows, vintage about 1990, so big and long that it looked as if there should be a third pair of wheels in the middle. Or maybe a helmsman way up on the back to steer, like those old hook-n-ladders used to have. Obviously not expecting to come so suddenly to a dead end road, it turned around as quickly as possible in the parking area only a hundred feet from us, paused a few seconds for the occupants to get a good look at us, then took off in a cloud of reddish brown dust. But Fiona had gotten a good look at it.

"Clive, it had a Georgia tag!" Then she shivered as she thought what that might mean.

I could have brushed it off as a coincidence, but I had glimpsed probably the same vehicle in the lot at Hoover Dam, and it almost certainly was the same one that had run Fiona down two nights ago. We were going to have to figure out what to do next, so we polished off the last of the wine, loaded the detritus in the car and headed on back to the hotel to work out a plan.

My impulse was to check out of the hotel and head East, waiting for nobody and no thing, but Fiona would have none of it. She was determined not to be panicked by some silly hobgoblin, and besides, she was determined to have at least one round of golf with me before we left. By the time I'd given in, we were back at our hotel. One plus I got out of it was that she very much wanted me to check out of my room and spend the night with her. I wasn't a professional bodyguard, but just having me there would make

79

her more comfortable. Who was I to disagree with a plan as sensible as that?

If I ever make a list of the best nights of my life, this one would be on page one up close to the top. Whatever it was that had been so good and special for us before, came back in spades. It's hard to describe this kind of magic, or to explain how something can suddenly be so right after a few bad years, but there it was. We made love with tenderness and enough passion to make us forget all about big black cars with the wrong kind of license plates, and even to forget that Fiona was still a suspect in what I had already classified as justifiable homicide. And then we went to sleep in each other's arms and didn't wake up until Mr. Sun looked into our window and winked at us. That's how we knew it was Sunday. We had black coffee and Danish at the little kitchen table, still in our robes, and I'm thinking Golf, and the sooner the better. But Fiona was thinking something else.

"Clive, can we go to church this morning?"

"Sure, honey, if you want to. But frankly, there's not a whole lot I need to pray for this morning, unless it's an eagle on that short par five across the water, and I doubt if God is even going to listen to that."

"Mr. Trebor, it's people like you who give praying a bad name. You can pray in thanksgiving for things, too. Has anything good happened to you recently that is worth giving thanks for?"

She had me there, so I agreed that we should do it. I figured it might do me some good, and sure couldn't hurt. And it might give us a leg up on that nasty infidel in the big black car. I was confident *he* wasn't going to church this morning, although I had read somewhere that 99% of the traveling public attend a church or synagogue when away from home on Saturday or Sunday.

My Dad had once told me that before planning a trip you should consult the long-range weather forecast, and select a weekend when rain and general all-round climatological nastiness portends. In that way, you can be sure that the place of worship you attend will have ample room in the pews for visitors. Furthermore, those present will more closely approximate your own dedication and saintliness.

It was too late for that now, but I could take his advice on further precautions.

80

"Fiona, as we both know, there are damn near as many churches in Las Vegas as there are gambling joints, and a number of them are within a short walk of this very hotel. Our problem is to select the right one."

"What do you mean?"

"I suggest entering the first convenient House of God, and taking a gander at the program."

"What then?" she asked, deciding to go with the flow of yet another probably ill-fated Trebor Master Plan.

"Well, suppose we see that the pastor is not giving the sermon, but rather there is to be a special pageant put on by the sixth-grade boys Sunday School class?"

"So what?"

"So, you might just go along with it; but I'm one of those wretched souls without the intellectual and emotional maturity to appreciate cultural Nirvana, so I'd suggest that we leave it and go on to the next prospect."

"Clive, that's the dumbest thing I ever heard. I have already picked out the church; it's one I've been to before."

"O.K., so we're over the hurdle, but how about the other pitfalls? Like when the congregation recites aloud the Lord's Prayer, and you come to that place where you ask for forgiveness. I never know whether to use the word 'debts,' like some Protestant Churches, or 'sins' like some others, or maybe 'trespasses.' Of course, all this is done to allow the local folks to identify the aliens. Like me. I always have a feeling that's exactly what they're doing, and looking into the black depths of my wretched soul to boot."

Fiona only smiled at this like you do at a not-too-bright child. But I was getting pretty wound up, and wasn't going to quit while I was behind.

"And singing is a tricky business if you are a card-carrying monotone such as I. I've tried a lot of tactics, but haven't had much success."

"What tactics, poor Clive?"

"Well, often I'd just silently mouth the words, but that seemed kind of cowardly. I once tried staying seated with head in hands as if sick, but that got mother upset. And a number of times I've remained defiantly silent with my lips compressed, but too many

81

people looked at me like I was mad at God. As an adult my routine has been just to sing, however badly, and keep glaring at any timid soul nearby on every sour note, in hopes of transferring the blame."

Fiona got a thoughtful look on her face like maybe she should go it alone this morning; but then she shook her head defiantly as if to say that she would suffer any mortification to get this sinner into church. "Don't worry, Clive, but try not to attract any attention."

I was just about to tell her about the stomach gurgles, but thought better of it. For reasons beyond the ken of mere mortals, I always got the gurgles during moments of silent prayer. Since I didn't have the control and training of an elderly acquaintance of mine, who could play "Rock of Ages" with her digestive tract, my stomach sometimes pushed me to the brink of serious mortification. Rather than try to explain this to Fiona now, I'd cope with it if it happened. I figured maybe the best thing to do would be to try to transfer the blame (as explained above under singing problems).

But there was still the "Stand Up and Be Recognized" ordeal to reckon with.

"Fiona, did I tell you about the time in college when I tried to make points with my snooty date and her parents by asking to go to church with them?"

"No, you haven't, but I have this sinking feeling you're going to," she offered, mildly disgusted at my foot-dragging tactics.

Ignoring her sarcasm, I continued, "Everything was cool until the preacher asked any visitors to stand up and tell their names and where they were from."

"Surely you could handle that!" my True Love exploded.

"Yeah, I wasn't too worried until this distinguished gentleman who preceded me turned a sickly green and introduced himself as 'Job Bones from Yew Nork.' That shook me a tad, but I could still handle it. Then I suddenly realized that I'd been asked to 'tell us a little something about yourself.'"

"That caused you a problem?" Fiona asked incredulously.

"You might say. In a daze I started out with my place and date of birth, and was just getting to my third grade education, when it dawned on me from the hostile stares that perhaps they didn't really want to know *that much* about me."

"Fiona," I said resolutely, "if I'm confronted with that challenge this morning, I will ignore it and mutter to my near neighbors something along the lines of 'Sure are a lot of visitors today.' "

She just laughed at me and said that they didn't do that at this church, and I'd be fine, so don't worry. With that we headed out to the Second Reformed Church of the Forgiveness of Sins.

Everything went well until they passed the collection plate. I know the ropes. The rule is that you fold a one or five dollar bill so it can't be identified by the formidable lady next to you with lorgnette, while a twenty or a fifty can be tossed in the plate with the large numbers in plain view. But real pros know that big contributors mail in a check on a monthly or quarterly basis, so the preferred ploy is to pass the plate along with a smug look and no contribution. I proceeded to do same, but Fiona gave a look of Total Disgust that will probably appear in The Guiness Book of Records for that category, grabbed the plate and deposited a Ten of her own therein. That halo I'd earned for being in the Holy Place suddenly seemed more like a noose which was about to slip down and strangle the sin out of my unworthy self.

When we emerged without further embarrassments, the bright sun came to my rescue by making Fiona forget my transgression and focus on our upcoming golf game. Suited me fine. We grabbed a quick bite at the hotel, changed clothes, piled our clubs and selves in the Hup, and headed for the Calloused Concubine where Big John Hurt had arranged a tee time for the three of us.

I liked the new John Hurt a lot better than that mean old bastard from days gone by. Rather than intrude on some private fun that Fiona and I were going to enjoy this Sunday afternoon, Big John added to the party. It was a pleasure to watch his smooth powerful swing, and it was amazing to see him smile and shake his head ruefully when he missed a short putt. No more swearing and club throwing like in the bad old days. Friend John was indeed a new man.

As good as it was to watch Hurt, it was a hundred times more fun to watch Fiona, because her equally smooth swing was augmented by plus factors that John wasn't born with. I kind of got caught up in the thing, and raised my own game a notch or too. Never had so much fun without a bet or a prize to go for.

I'd never seen Fiona hit her irons any crisper, and those babies were really checking up on the greens, usually spinning back a few feet to boot. But when we came to the eighteenth hole, her drive was off the fairway and into the wet rough where a sprinkler had worked a little overtime. She came out with a beautiful eight-iron to the green, and that crazy thing actually backed up ten feet after it landed.

"John, did you see that, out of the wet grass?"

"Yeah," he said, "I didn't know she was playing with square grooves."

All of a sudden the afternoon turned to ashes, as the words of Phineas Physis invaded my rapidly-numbing mind: ". . . . the lethal club had square grooves."

I uncharacteristically chili-dipped my approach shot and ended with my first bogie of the day, giving thanks that it was the last hole. Somehow I managed to keep my emotions under control, thanked John, and drove back to the Hotel with Fiona.

She was so happy with the gaudy 67 she'd posted that she didn't notice my sudden lack of small talk on the way back, and when we got to her room the first thing she wanted was a long hot bath. This gave me more time to think. First thing was to verify that she did have square grooves. A quick trip down to the garage and a look at her clubs in the trunk of the car affirmed that this was so.

Back in the room, the next step was to pour a straight bourbon to grease the wheels of cogitation. After about 15 minutes of internal struggle, my brain decided that square grooves didn't really prove anything, lots of top golfers used them. All doubts were pushed far enough back into the remote regions of my mind to allow me to act normal when Fiona came out of her bath, and in fifteen or twenty minutes I'd forgotten everything except how much I loved this woman.

Next morning was time to hit the road for Savannah, and what might await us there. We hadn't yet planned our itinerary, but the first leg had to be to Colorado Springs to confer with some of

B.B.'s criminologist friends. At his request, these computer mavens had been running searches on all sorts of murder cases in which golf clubs were involved. In our last phone conversation Tolliver had opined that "as long as I was in that neighborhood, I could check up on their results."

I pointed the Hup onto I-15, and she ate up the 300 miles to the I-70 cutoff like it was a short drive in the country. We hadn't stopped yet to eat, because the laws which created our vast Interstate Highway System provided that it would be illegal to operate a decent restaurant within five miles of the highway. However, by this time the old gut was rumbling up a storm, just begging me to do something about it, so we exited the Interstate and headed for the nearest small town. Fiona had a theory on finding a good restaurant.

"Clive, I've heard that the thing to do is look for where all the trucks are parked. The drivers are on the road constantly, and experience has taught them where the good food is."

I was amazed that someone who had been around as much as she should still believe in fairy tales.

"Dear one," I said, "Most of those semi jockeys have been on the road so long that they're dreaming of something, and it's not food. Show me a diner with a lot of trucks parked out front and I'll show you a joint with a waitress with too much bust wearing too little to keep it from busting out."

"Well, maybe we should stop there anyway, Stud. A little selective viewing might get your system circulating, too."

I ignored any insult that might have been implied by that last statement, and completed my observations on roadside dining. "Madam, I make it a practice to avoid diners connected to service stations because they clean the dishes with gasoline. Furthermore I will not set foot in a restaurant called 'Mom's' because I'm not all that fond of the vegetarian plate, particularly if Mom chides me for not eating the broccoli."

We solved the eating problem by stopping at a medium-sized food market with a built-in deli department, and picked up some pastrami sandwiches and Coors. It wasn't quite a New York deli, but the sandwiches were OK, and Coors is Coors wherever it's served. Then it was on to I-70 for a straight shot through increasingly beautiful mountain scenery into Grand Junction.

We found a comfortable motel for the night, and as soon as we checked in I called B.B. Tolliver's office in Savannah. The night man answered, and when I identified myself, he promised to locate B.B. as soon as possible. We went down the street to a steak joint, and enjoyed a couple of sirloins from real Colorado cows. We got back to our room just in time to answer the phone.

"This is Tolliver. That you, Clive?"

I confessed that it was. I quickly told him about the big black Lincoln town car that had hit Fiona, and was still trailing us, probably with malice aforethought.

"B.B., can you get a list of Soundings residents who drive black late-model Lincoln town cars?"

"Surely you jest. There are more of those big boats at The Soundings than there are Fords and Chevys."

"Okay, partner, I guess I knew that. How about just checking the suspects we talked about?"

"Can do, Clive. And I'll nose around to see if any of them have turned up missing the past few days."

I thanked him, and agreed to call him the following afternoon from Colorado Springs. Fiona and I spent the rest of the evening getting further acquainted, before hitting the sack in preparation for an early start next morning.

We had a pleasant uneventful trip through the mountains, and pulled into Colorado Springs early in the afternoon. We had already decided to suspend the budget for two nights to stay at the incomparable Broadmoor. It had too many fond memories for us to forego, even considering the anemic state of my bankroll. We were lucky to be able to get a room with a fine mountain view in the newer building across the pond.

First order of business was to phone Savannah. Tolliver was waiting for me, and he wasted no time getting to the point.

"Only one Town Car owner turned up in thuh whole passel o'folks we're watching. I'm talkin' 'bout Winthrop Winchester hisself."

"No kidding! And next you're going to tell me he's been out of town the last few days."

"Bing-o. And tuh make thuh cheese more bindin', thuh old boy who lives next tuh old Winnie spotted him pullin' out of his driveway just about the time you took off for Palm Springs. Nobody's seen hide nor hair of him since, and there ain't no vehicle in his gay-rahge."

B.B.'s exaggerated accent betrayed the excitement he felt at this first real breakthrough we'd had thus far. I shared his excitement, but in my case it was mixed with relief that the unknown menace was now exposed. I had a fair amount of confidence that I could deal with that old windbag just about any day of the week in any state from Colorado to Georgia. And I really looked forward to finding out what he was up to. If he meant any further harm to Fiona, I'd make sure he'd never bore the audience at the Neebrace Racquet Club again.

B.B. supplied Winchester's license plate number, YYX-123, and rang off with the admonition to be careful. I turned to Fiona, and filled her in on any of the conversation she hadn't been able to deduce from listening to my half of it.

"Clive, I don't really know Winchester. I heard Barry mention his name a few times, because they were apparently pretty good tennis friends."

This interesting comment verified that Dorothy LaMoste had totally fabricated the feud between Brasher and Winchester. I couldn't imagine why. Also, I was in the dark as to why Winchester had run down Fiona, who didn't even know him. It is at this point when the brilliant investigator is supposed to say Eureka or something like that, showing that he has fitted together all the pieces of the puzzle. I didn't even know if we'd identified all the pieces.

It was too late for a few holes of golf, but never too late to visit that great little bar in the basement of the stately old hotel building. There was a friendly but manageable-sized crowd at the bar, and Fiona and I decided to have a little fun with the old game we used to play there some eons ago. The game would be on if there were only two single empty seats and there was one guy in between them and we wanted to get him to move without actually asking. This particularly evening we peeked through the door and found that conditions were 'Go,' and this is how it went:

Fiona entered first, sat down next to the potential victim at the bar, and ordered a drink. I then came in and occupied the stool on his other side.

"Excuse me, Lady," I opened, talking right across his bow to Fiona, "I know this sounds corny, but I truly believe I've met you, and can't remember where or when."

"You're right," she replied, also right across the victim's bow, "it is corny; but you do look vaguely familiar."

"Did you ever go to O'Flaherty's in New York?" I asked her.

Fiona watched our victim surreptitiously, and seeing no reaction, replied, "Never."

Then she spoke up again, "I'm sure I've seen you, and I feel like it was more than once. How about the Playboy Club on Lake Geneva?"

Again there was no reaction from the gentleman in the middle of our crossfire, so I replied in the negative.

At about this point the majority of our victims are ready to give up, and offer to move over so that we can sit together and talk to our hearts' content. Our objective is then accomplished, but without much fun. Fortunately our man tonight was made of sterner stuff, and hung in there, but it was obvious that he was following our conversation with interest.

I began again, "I used to live in Minneapolis," and as our man almost jumped out of his skin, it looked like we were getting somewhere.

Fiona caught it and reacted quickly, "I spent a few years there myself. Did you ever go to Lord Fletcher's on the Lake?"

His reaction told me we had him. I replied excitedly to Fiona, "Sure did; went there all the time."

We both paused, and the guy in the middle couldn't help himself. "I went there a few times myself!"

We both looked at him. "Yeah," I said, "It's all coming back to me now. You were there and introduced me to *her*," nodding with loathing at Fiona. "That's when my trouble began."

Our victim had spunk. "I've never seen either one of you people before," he said, "and I hope I never see you again."

With that he chug-a-lugged the rest of his drink, got up and walked out. I moved over to his vacated seat, and Fiona and I drank to another successful ploy.

The bartender interrupted our orgy of self-congratulation: "Your buddy left without paying for his drinks. That's five-fifty, Mac."

"But," I sputtered, "he's not our buddy; we never saw him before."

This drew a snort from our friendly publican. "Come off it, Mac. I heard the three of you talking about all those bars you used to hang out at. Your buddy had two scotch and sodas, and that's five-fifty."

Fiona looked at me sweating and fuming and almost busted out laughing. "Pay the man, Clyde, he's got you."

What could I do? I paid the man. But I did get the last word: "For your information, my name's not Clyde, and I still don't know the guy."

By the time we finished our drinks, I could see the humor in the situation, and decided to relax and enjoy it. We had great lamp chops in the dining room and walked in the moonlight back to our building on the other side of the lagoon. Things only got better back in our room.

Next morning, I headed downtown to an office which said "Attorneys At Law" on the door, but was really a front for a special branch of the FBI who did all sorts of things that Headquarters in Washington didn't want to be associated with. I identified myself and asked to see Mr. Dunn, who was B.B.'s contact. After being palmed off from one bored official to another for at least an hour, I was told that Mr. Dunn had been transferred to Washington, along with his work load which included B.B.'s project. No, no one else could discuss it with us. Yes, we would have to go to Washington to confer with Dunn himself.

All the way back to the Broadmoor I fumed about Bureaucracy, and how little they cared if someone came all the way to Colorado on a wild goose chase. I was still a little miffed when I got B.B. on the phone, and it didn't help my disposition when he insisted that I come home via Washington since it was "on the way." Could he really be that poor in Geography?

Fiona calmed me down immediately by pointing out that it was a little late in the day to be starting on the road, so the only logical thing to do was to check and see if the golf courses were in good playing condition. Turned out they were.

The next day we headed East, planning to spend the first night in Topeka and the second in Louisville. That way we wouldn't be all worn out when we reached Washington on the third evening.

We got a fairly early start because we had a long boring drive ahead of us, but Fiona managed to down three cups of coffee before we left. That might portend serious problems later on for a neophyte driver, but Old Clive had been on the road enough times to handle a simple little situation like this. As we headed out of The Springs on U.S. 24, I made a note to myself that we would encounter no Rest Stops until we reached I-70 more than an hour away. I kept my fingers crossed, but heard not a peep from my traveling companion. As soon as we reached the Interstate, I immediately began watching for signs telling how many miles to the next rest stop, and was soon rewarded: "Rest Area 2 Miles." I was ready to pull in, because seasoned travelers never pass up an opportunity to go to the bathroom, but Fiona wanted to know why we were stopping so soon. We pressed on. Right after we passed a sign saying the next Rest Area was 73 miles away, my True Love informed me that nature was calling and she was going to have to answer ASAP.

"Fiona, why didn't you want to stop at that rest area six minutes ago?"

"I didn't need to go then."

I didn't feel it was wise to carry the interrogation any further, but I was reminded of the strategy of one of my married friends when traveling with their kids: he stopped every 100 miles and spanked them all whether they needed it or not. I was pretty sure Fiona wouldn't appreciate being likened to children, and I was *real* sure my friend's strategy would not work in this case.

So, of course, I did what I could, which was to pull off the interstate at the next small town and find a Gas Station. Having filled the tank just before leaving Colorado Springs, I managed to squeeze in just $3.29 worth of gas. When I asked the manager for the key to the rest room, he muttered something about planning to put in a pay toilet for cheapskate freeloaders from out of state. Fortunately, Fiona came in the door about then, smiled at him, and took the key from his limp grip. He was still staring as she disappeared down the back hall.

Back on the road, I began to fume and fuss at having to beg for admittance to the toilet after having bought so little gas, but

Fiona looked at me sweetly and said, "Clive dear, all seasoned travelers know you should leave enough freeboard in the gas tank to make a reasonable purchase at any unscheduled pit stop."

The score was now: Fiona-999, Clive-0.

But just being in the car with the once and future love of my life was enough to revive my spirits, and I was even able to enjoy some of the most utterly boring scenery on this continent all the way to Topeka. We got in about five that evening, and found a motel on the east side of town with room rates low enough to slightly compensate for our excesses at the Broadmoor. After a couple of drinks and dinner at an undistinguished Italian restaurant down the street we came back to the room to settle down for the evening. Fiona got involved in a TV program, a rerun of "Murder, She Wrote," starring Angela Lansbury. Angela is one of my favorite actresses, but I had already seen this particular episode, and I wasn't ready to settle down quite yet.

Leaving my roomie to help Angela solve the case, I strolled down the street past all the motels and gas stations and fast food shops to where an adjoining residential area began. I had already turned around to go back when I got this uneasy feeling that I was being observed by someone. I stopped as if to look in a store window and caught the reflection of a large black sedan going past at a snail's pace. It was indeed a Lincoln Towncar, and the gray tinted windows kept me from seeing who was in it. But I would swear that I glimpsed the tell-tale peach of the State of Georgia on the tag as it went by in the semi-darkness. So we were still being followed, and ten would get you one that it was His Windbagness Winthrop Winchester who was doing the following.

I decided not to say anything to Fiona about this, as I couldn't see that getting both of us uptight was any big improvement over just me having the jitters. And so to bed.

We were on the road early next morning, and Fiona graciously refrained from having her customary three cups of java, probably in the interest of keeping me sane. Aside from the interesting spectacle of hawks perched on 27% of the fence posts, the Kansas Turnpike from Topeka to Kansas City is notable for maximally repetitive terrain. Not being gifted with an appreciation for the poetic beauty of Your Nation's Agriculture At Work Providing

Bread for A Hungry World, I feel that if you've seen one wheat field you've seen them all.

But I had to admit that things had changed significantly for the better since my last trek along this highway. On that occasion, you couldn't have looked at the scenery if there had been some; your total concentration being focused on dodging cavernous mega-potholes. And worse yet, some economy-minded politico in Topeka had thought to save money by awarding the restaurant franchise to the lowest bidder, resulting in a world-class stretch of ptomaine breeding ground with a largely captive audience to work on. Happily, this situation has also been alleviated, and I hope it stays that way for my next trip through this fair state.

Now you're probably thinking that I am, or have been, anti-Kansas or something, and it may be true, but I'm definitely not anti-*Kansans*. I know of no better class of honest, forthright and likeable people in the entire country, and it's too bad that so many travelers have formed this negative opinion of them when passing briefly through during bad highway years. Heck, the Kansans have had to fight the potholes and eat the rotten food every day of the year.

But we persisted, and soon crossed the river into one of the really nice cities in the whole Midwest, Kansas City, Missouri. Of course this is just another cross the Jayhawks have to bear, having a great city with their name hooked to it belong to some other state.

10.

At any rate, we arrived in Louisville, KY late in the afternoon, and drove on through to the eastern suburbs to find a motel well on the way to Lexington, so as to not get caught in rush hour traffic next morning.

I pulled into the Alldun Inn, a relatively new establishment which hadn't had time to achieve the rundown and shabby decor exhibited by many of the older chains. The young man at the desk was too friendly and polite to have been on the job for more than a couple of weeks. Heck, he hadn't been on this earth for too many years, judging by the embryo mustache which needed at least another year's growth to be respectable. Just the kind of room clerk I like to meet when I'm on a tight budget.

"Yessir, may I help you?"

"I'd like a room for two, king-size bed, first floor."

"No problem," he said, after checking the computer screen. "The rate will be $55.00."

"I'm sure you have a corporate rate. My Leviathon Corp. number is LC 696900."

I had obtained this identification number by eavesdropping on a Dark Gray Suit who was registering just ahead of me one night at the Airport Hilton near San Francisco about five years ago. It has worked for me ever since, and not only at hostelries, but also at rent-a-cars and florists shops. I think I'm going to try it in church some day. I have told Fiona about this, (the motel part, not the church part), and she grudgingly allows me to do it.

The young clerk obviously hadn't run across this particular corporation before, and he wasn't sure just how to look it up. I could see the gears grinding in his thinking machine, then come to a major decision.

"Yessir, that rate will be fifty instead of fifty-five."

He handed me the room key and wished me a happy evening. I was pretty sure I'd get another five bucks off when I checked out in the morning, just by flashing my Preferred Customer card for the Alldun Inn Motel chain. I'd noticed that when he typed up the room invoice, he hadn't made any note about a corporate rate, and I'd be very surprised if he communicated anything to the day clerk who relieved him.

After dinner, I was feeling restless, and my regular ritual of push-ups, knee-bends and a dozen other exercises taught me by Otsuki, was not enough to relax mind and body.

"Fiona, how about taking a little stroll to work out the kinks?"

"Why don't you go on by yourself? There's a TV special I want to watch."

She didn't mention the name of the show, because she knew my TV appetite was mostly for sports programs, but I knew it was the Oscar Awards or the Emmy Awards, or some other type of awesomely boring awards.

"Maybe I will go out for a breath of air. If I'm lucky, and the wind is blowing in the right direction, it might even be moderately fresh air."

She nodded without really hearing me, because some little guy with too much makeup and too loud a voice was proclaiming the millenium, awards-wise, that is.

I got through the door without throwing up, and started down the driveway toward the back. With the big black sedan image of the previous night firmly in mind, I began to scout around for a possible sighting of same tonight. It occurred to me that our shadower might even be checked in at our motel; it was big enough to make it unlikely for us to run into him by accident. With this thought, I walked clear around the sprawling establishment to the far side, where a new addition had recently been made, and the driveway had not yet even been paved. There were a couple of cars parked there, but nothing big or black or Lincoln or towncar. As I was just about to go around the far corner of the building, a car entered the gravel driveway and pulled up in front of one of the rooms. The size and color of the vehicle immediately alerted me, and the gaudy Georgia tag with the number YYX-123 nailed it down. It was Winchester. As he got out of the car in the dim light, I was surprised at his size. I had only seen him the one time, sitting behind a table at the Neebrace Racquet Club, and had a picture of him in my mind as an average-sized guy of athletic build. I had it half right; he definitely was built like an athlete, and moved like one. But this guy had at least 225 lbs of bone and gristle under his control, and probably hadn't ever had an ounce of fat on his six-foot-two frame.

Still, I kept moving toward him, because I had on occasion run into some big ones and some strong ones, and none of them had been a match for the arcane skills I'd learned from my Japanese mentor so long ago. I had work to do, and I was going to do it now.

I wasn't more than ten feet away when something caused him to look back, and his face showed surprise as he recognized me. "Trebor, you rotten sonavabitch!"

The derogatory salutation didn't bother me, but the way he dropped into a crouch facing me with feet spread and hands slightly apart in front of his face wasn't any cause for celebration. He hadn't learned that playing doubles with the old ladies at the

94

racquet club, and my mind registered that I wasn't facing some wild-swinging pushover.

His features contorted as he snarled, "Come on closer, boy, and I'll show you how we did things in the 114th Infantry!"

That revelation wasn't exactly the best news I'd heard all week, but it did give me a clue as to how he might fight. I noticed his eyes flick briefly to the bare ground and gravel beneath us, and I knew what he was thinking. Even so, he moved so quickly he almost caught me. The handful of dirt and gravel he scooped up mostly sailed by my head as I lunged sharply to the left and in toward his body. In hurling this stuff at my face, he hoped to blind me, at least for the second or two it would take him to land a killing blow. But the risk he took, as I well knew, was that the act of throwing would cause him to straighten up out of his protective crouch. In the milliseconds he was thus exposed I aimed a vicious kick at his family jewels. I definitely struck him somewhere hard enough to cause him to gasp and pull back, but since he didn't scream in pain I knew I hadn't landed on Target A.

Apparently my foot had caught some of his hipbone, which didn't bother him, but had also registered in the area where the appendix was supposed to be, and this did bother him considerably. But he was still on his feet and looking menacing, and he now realized that he wasn't playing with a cub scout, which gave him enough wariness to be even more dangerous.

We circled around each other, neither one wanting to initiate anything that would allow the other to find an opening. It didn't take me all that long to see that I was going to have to come up with something pretty quick, and I was almost sure it was going to fall in the category of "no pain: no gain." I just hoped that most of the pain would be for Winny and most of the gain for yours truly. So, ever optimistic, I went into the old False Trip ploy. With this expert a foe, it couldn't be overdone or he would be suspicious. The idea was to feign tripping and falling off balance, and sidestepping his inevitable attack just enough to catch him in a vulnerable spot with one of my own weapons. As the British say in all the old movies when something is resolved, "Done and done."

Unfortunately, I'd never tried this before on anyone as expert as Winchester. As I pretended to trip and stagger, he threw a vicious right cross so fast that I couldn't completely sideslip it, and it caught me an only-partially glancing blow on my left ear. I heard all one hundred bells of the Alpine Chorus at once, and I wasn't able to even start my own counterblow. As I stumbled backward, I knew that I had to do something impressive real fast, because in a prolonged fight he would make mincemeat of me.

The plan I came up with in the next microsecond did not win any applause from my already aching head bone, but it was the best chance I had: I would take another shot from Winthrop to make him think he had me.

I staggered as if he had really dizzied me, and waited for his reaction. It wasn't long in coming, but this time I had his motion figured out a little better so that his big right fist smacked off my left hand which was covering the side of my face. The impact sounded loud and brutal. I started to go down, and he forgot caution in his attempt to finish me off for good. He shouldn't have done it. I deftly sidestepped his rush, and drove my rigid extended fingers into his solar plexus. As he folded in the middle, I gave him a short sharp chop with the heel of my left hand across his Adam's apple, holding back enough to reduce the odds of killing him outright. Before he could fall to the ground, I brought my knee up sharply into his groin area, this last being a down payment on what he owed for running down Fiona in Las Vegas.

Winston groaned loudly, made a few gurgling noises as he threw up all over his lemon yellow slacks, and finally lay still in the gravel. He wouldn't be talking for the next few minutes, but I could wait.

Just as I finished a cursory examination of my person and concluded that a swollen ear and a slight headache was the extent of the damage, the door to the nearest room opened and the shape of a large person was silhouetted in the light from the room. This large person was female, had red hair, and went by the name of Dorothy LaMoste. However, what she was holding in her hand was not the customary DuBonnet, but a .38 caliber snub nose revolver. It was pointed at me.

"Very impressive, Clive," said Dorothy, "you're even better at that than you are in bed. Pray bring poor Winchester in here before he catches his death, if he hasn't already."

As instructed, I dragged the unconscious man into the room, and Dorothy closed the door. I was fascinated at her lack of concern for Winchester, but even more bewildered by the turn of events.

Before I could begin to ask questions, Dorothy said, apologetically, "Clive I'm really sorry about the last few days. I'll put this gun down as soon as I'm convinced that you'll behave."

How was she going to insure that? Tie me up? Drug me?

Always quick with sparkling repartee, I asked, "Who are you really, and what's this all about?"

To her credit, Dorothy didn't laugh at my preposterous cliche. Instead she got a thoughtful look on her beautiful face, struggled a little with her better judgement and seemed to win the struggle. "Clive, I'm going to tell you everything, and I'm going to trust you not to let it go any further than it has to."

An interesting beginning. I said as much.

My interruption didn't faze her; heck I don't think she even heard me. "Clive, I work for a special branch of the Narcotics Division of the U.S. Treasury Department. About a year ago I went to Savannah to straighten out a bad situation in our field office, and to get a fresh reading on rumors that Colombian Drug Dealers were starting a big push in Georgia and South Carolina. I started making real progress just a few weeks ago."

She paused, and I couldn't resist filling the silence. "What has that got to do with me?"

"What I thought it had to do with you was a concrete coffin, or at best a long vacation at Uncle Sam's little rest resort up the Hudson at Ossining, New York. That is, I thought that up to about thirty minutes ago."

This time I had enough sense to shut up and wait for her to continue.

"We'd been tipped that a big drug boss had arrived in the area, and was going to spend enough time in Savannah to get things organized. He was supposed to get into town the very night you came floating in on the Greyhound bus. His description matched yours extremely well, and we had a blurry picture of him that could very well have been you. It may be the mustache, Clive-o, but you could pass for Hispanic even in Cartagena. At any rate we were preparing to bust you under the Drug Kingpin statute."

"You must have known I was working with the police."

"Correction. We knew you were working with one policeman, and a bit of a weirdo at that. You have to admit that Billy Bob Tolliver is not your average everyday flatfoot. We figured he's been turned, and was in the smuggling deal with you. We really got excited when we found out he had dispatched you to Palm Springs and Las Vegas. Looked like a big new network was being set up."

"How did you learn where I was headed and how did you find me in Las Vegas so quickly?"

"Answer to question number one is that we had our own informer in the State police, and they were coordinating things with Tolliver's superiors. Answer to question number two is the big old car. You couldn't hide from a blind man in that ancient rolling stock. Soon as we found out your travel plans, Winchester and I hopped in that big land cruiser of his and burned rubber for Las Vegas to intercept you. Meantime, our agent in Palm Springs followed you to that house you visited, and saw you leave in the old car. It was duck soup to locate you in Vegas. I figured you'd put that baby in a garage, and we found it in the third place we looked."

"What has Winchester got to do with all of this?"

"He was in charge of our Savannah office. He'd gotten into booze too heavy, and I was sent down to straighten him out. A real sad case. He'd been one of the best until the Demon Rum got his number. Very sharp, great actor, well trained, knew the ropes, and one formidable sonavabitch in a scuffle, as you may have noticed. In fact you're maybe the first guy he ever finished second to in an unfair fight."

This was said with at least a trace of admiration, which I tried unsuccessfully to ignore. But any little ego boost I'd gotten out of that was quickly forgotten in anger at my recollection of what had happened in Las Vegas.

"Dorothy, why did you try to run me down the other night; is that standard procedure for suspected drug dealers?"

"Stupid as it sounds, that was a pure accident. We had just caught your trail, and were following at a discreet distance behind you. Unknown to me, Winchester had been hitting the bottle, and his judgement was impaired. He gunned the motor to pass you. I tried to stop him to keep from blowing our cover, and in the struggle and confusion he lost control of the steering wheel and we were up on the sidewalk. We must have traveled three hundred feet before he could get it back onto the street."

"But not before you damned near killed Fiona!" I snarled.

"Clive, what are you talking about?" Dorothy asked, and the look on her face told me she didn't really know.

I explained what had happened. She was really shaken. She hadn't even known that Fiona was in Las Vegas until they spotted her with me two days later at Lake Meade.

"I'm so sorry. Is she OK now?"

"Yes, but no thanks to the zombie on the bed there. That's inexcusable, what he did. I've been known to have a drink now and then, but not when I'm going to drive. As a taxpayer I'd say the quicker we retire that Civil Servant the better. But never mind that. You intimated that I'm no longer a drug suspect. What's the story?"

"Not thirty minutes ago I got a call from the big boys in D.C. They caught the real drug smuggler in Charleston, and they've got the goods on him. They say it's amazing how much he looks like your picture. But as far as Winchester is concerned, I agree with you; I don't see how I can recommend that he keep his job."

As she finished speaking, we heard a couple of groans from the direction of the bed, and Winchester sat up and looked at us. "God, LaMoste, that's not fair," he croaked. "I haven't had a drink since that night in Vegas, and as far as hitting a woman with the car, that was mostly your fault for grabbing the steering wheel."

Then he turned in my direction. "I heard what Dorothy said about you being innocent of the drug charge, and I guess you figure I owe you an apology. You can forget it, you bastard. You may be clear with Her Nibs here, and with those stupid paper pushers in our Nation's Fair Capital, but I still figure you're guilty as hell. And I don't appreciate the little extra treatment you dished out after you got lucky in that little scuffle we had. It's bad enough to have my voice box ruined and my sternum seriously in pain, but why the knee in the groin? You know you already had me."

"Well, Winchester, it's true that the last touch I applied was unnecessary; but I looked at it as just the first payment you were going to make for hitting Fiona. And you've got to remember that I figured you to be a probable murderer. Anyway, even if you didn't try to hit Fiona you're to blame. No, I'm not sorry."

Dorothy decided to put in her oar to cool things down. "OK Winthrop, I'll decide what to tell the Bureau later; but I can't fault Clive for what he did. The bright spot is that you're probably off the hook as far as being a murder suspect." Then she said to me. "That's right, isn't it Clive?"

Before I could answer, Winchester was off the bed and at the door giving us both a parting shot. "I'll get you for this, you frigging beanpole. And you too, you mean bitch." He slammed the door to punctuate his words, and in a minute we heard the roar of the big Lincoln as it blasted out of the parking lot, throwing gravel up against the door as it went.

We waited a minute or too for the dust to settle, then Dorothy spoke up. "Clive, don't worry about him and his threats. He's mostly bluff, and he'll get over this soon enough."

I wasn't so sure. He seemed like one mean and vengeful character, and I wasn't 100% sure I could handle him next time push came to shove. But there wasn't anything I could do about it at that point, and I had some more questions I wanted to ask Dorothy. She was still a suspect in the Brasher murder, and I was worried about her animosity toward Fiona as well.

"Dorothy, what was with you and Barry Brasher?"

"Well Clive, it was really regrettable. I met him at the Oleander Club, and I thought him attractive. You'd be surprised how charming that SOB could be when he wanted something. We did spend a couple of nights together until I found out that he was married."

"I heard it lasted longer than that."

"Brasher did that. He found out he wasn't going to get much money from Fiona and he wanted out. He spread the story about me and him to provoke her to divorce. Looks like it worked."

"How about you and me?"

She smiled. "That gets complicated. I started out just to get information from you, at the same time you were trying to pump me. I really got some jollies from that situation, you thinking you were the great big cat, when all the time you were the mouse. But pretty soon I started to like you much too much, and it was getting to be a struggle to remember that you were the loathsome drug smuggler. I was getting ready to ask Washington to take me off the case, when you took off for Palm Springs and Las Vegas. Just my luck to find out you're one of the good guys after you've found your lost lover." She sighed.

"Yes, my lost lover." But I didn't sigh. "What about the big brouhaha with her?"

"With her AND Brasher. It was real. She was mad at me because she thought I was a marriage wrecker. I got mad because she wouldn't listen to my explanation, and of course we were both mad at Barry Bastard."

I thought the name appropriate. "Why did you lie about Winchester's supposed animosity toward Brasher?"

"Frankly I was afraid you'd learn that Winchester and I were working together. I thought a red herring might divert you from any such thoughts."

Yes, I thought, maybe you pointed me in his direction because he would be a suitable lamb for the supposed drug boss to slaughter. But I said nothing.

After a minute Dorothy said slowly, "Clive, you don't have to worry about me bothering you anymore. And our little romps in the hay will never come to Fiona's attention, at least not from me. I'm really sorry things turned out this way for us. Incidentally, I'm not mad at Fiona, and I hope someday we can be friends."

I felt like a heavy weight had been lifted. At least my relationship with Fiona wasn't threatened from this quarter. Now if only I could find the murderer and prove her innocent. . . .

Dorothy and I said goodbye. She was going to take a plane out to Savannah next morning. This time the kiss I gave her really was the kind you give your sister.

11.

When I came back into our motel room, Fiona was still watching the Awards program. I was dying to fill her in on the startling turn of events, but before I could get off the blocks, she flagged me down. They were about to present the award to the writer of The Best Situation Comedy Making Men Look Foolish, and Fiona didn't want to miss this biggie. I waited patiently for the next Commercial break before launching into my almost-unabridged account of the Adventures of Clive Trebor, protagonist in our particular David vs. Goliath potboiler. Not only did I have her full attention, she even pulled the plug on Hollywood-At-Its-Worst or whatever.

I recounted nearly everything that had happened, leaving out only the bit that was personal between Dorothy and me. I even told her that Dorothy wasn't to blame for her affair with Brasher, not knowing that he was married. Fiona said nothing, but when I told her that Ms. LaMoste hoped to be friends some day, Fiona's expression hardened, and she said only, "We'll see," through tightened lips. Always alert to the slightest nuance, Trebor-The-Sensitive perceived that they weren't going to be sorority sisters just yet.

Fiona became alarmed when I related Winchester's parting words of threat. She had all sorts of suggestions on saving my hide from this menace, ranging from cancelling the Washington leg of our journey to asking for police protection. With a show of confidence I didn't really feel, I quashed all her suggestions, assuring her that the old windbag was all Puff and no Stuff. We had a long trek ahead of us to Washington, so we turned in early in preparation for departure at dawn next day.

We proceeded without incident through the beautiful and once-formidable Appalachians, now largely tamed by the Interstate highway system. It was about six o'clock when we reached our destination, the old Shoreham hotel on Calvert St. overlooking Rock Creek Park. We had fond memories of this fine old land-mark, long since taken over by one of the big chains, and were looking forward to a couple of nights there. Fiona was devastated to learn from the doorman that there were no vacancies, and of course we had no reservation. I took it rather calmly, I thought, and assured my fellow traveller that Uncle Clive would take care of everything. Which I proceeded to do via the Johnson Phenomenon.

There are probably as many Johnsons in this country as there are Smiths or Joneses, but they are not subject to the same instant distrust that is accorded the latter two names. If you go to the desk of nearly any hotel or motel, and give your name as "John Jones," you'd better have your driver's license, your AARP card, your birth certificate and two character witnesses to prove your identity. But if you give your name as "Johnson," the clerk will probably say, "Yessir, we have reservations for a Phillip Johnson and a Malcolm Johnson; which one are you, sir?" Maybe everyone trusts Swedes.

At any rate Fiona and I were soon registered in good standing, and I didn't feel badly about the real Gunnar Johnson we had displaced, because when he arrived *he* would have proof of identity, and would get one of those rooms they always hold back for such emergencies. Knowing that Fiona's code of ethics was several light-years stricter than mine, I didn't crow over my cleverness, but merely told her that we had been lucky they had a cancellation.

The Shoreham wasn't exactly in the same price range as Motel Six or the The Red Roof, so compensatory frugality in the dining department was in order. I had a plan. Always on the lookout for really important events, as we walked through the lobby I had noticed that the hotel was currently playing host to The Pasta Growers Trade Show. One of the few worthwhile things I'd learned in my business career was how Trade Shows function, and particularly how Corporate Hospitality Suites work. It was his knowledge that I now put to good use.

"F, I know how we can wine and dine handsomely tonight at no cost and without leaving this fine Hostelry."

She looked at me suspiciously, and then as the light bulb went on in her head, suspicion turned to disgust. "Clive Trebor, we're not going to crash somebody's private party like we did that time in Chicago. I've never been so embarrassed in all my life."

"Well maybe that wasn't my finest hour; but it sure wasn't my fault that the water pitcher I was diluting my drink with was filled with Martinis. Anyway, this is The Pasta Growers convention, and I know a million of those guys from the old family business," I added, lying only a soupçon.

Fiona finally agreed to my scheme, but on condition that I "really did know all those people."

This ultimatum required a slight change in plans. The only guy I knew, who I could be sure would be in attendance, was Reggie Pemberton of Pemberton Pasta Pearls. Reggie was one of those versatile people who could be totally obnoxious in any social or business venue. He was a real pro. Nevertheless, we headed directly for the Pemberton suite, knowing that the booze would be cheap, the food minimal, and the company terminally boring. I figured one quick drink with Reggie would satisfy my promise to Fiona, and we could move on to a better world somewhere else in the hotel.

Done and done. Reggie hadn't improved, nor had the drink and food he proffered. To my delight it was Fiona who suggested moving on. The upshot is that just four doors down the hall we stumbled into a paradise for eaters and drinkers. What caught my eye as we passed their open door was the bar stock in plain view. Instead of Old Tennis Shoes or Grizzly Grog which are norm for many of these suites, I spied Wild Turkey representing the bourbon department, and correspondingly choice brands of scotch and gin. I propelled Fiona in ahead of me, without pausing to read the name of the host company in dignified small print on the door.

"Clive, are you sure you know these people?" she asked as her eyes pleasurably took in the jumbo shrimp, the smoked oysters, and the huge side of medium rare beef even now being carved before us.

"Of course," I replied, with as much assurance as I could muster, given the fact that I hadn't seen anyone I recognized SO FAR.

Heck, any moment now three or four of my old buddies would probably come out of the adjoining room to greet me. While waiting for this eventuality, no point letting all that good stuff spoil, and Wild Turkey is noted for its fast evaporation rate. Fiona was so occupied with the plethora of tasty viands that she forgot to follow up any further on her nagging duties, and we both had a rousing good time. True, I was a little puzzled at the several conversations I attempted to join. These people seemed to be interested in things like bridge supports, half crowns and the like. If I didn't know any better I would have thought we had wandered into an engineers' convention, but what the hay, they were all very friendly and made us feel at home.

When we finally said our farewells and were going out the door,

I got a good gander at that little sign I'd seen on the way in. I decided not to share what I read with Fiona, who even now was complimenting me on the quality of my friends and their lush spread. It might have taken a little edge off things if she knew that we had just crashed the Northern Virginia Dental Association's annual meeting.

Next morning I headed downtown to the address on 12th street where I had an appointment with the elusive Mr. Dunn, who had evaded me in Colorado Springs, but who had promised to share his expertise with me here in Washington. It was quite an ordinary three story office building, and Dunn occupied a small office on the top floor. A pleasant young man probably in his late twenties, casually dressed in polo shirt, corduroy slacks and sandals, ushered me in and offered me a seat in a well-experienced wicker chair. I could see that there were no adjoining rooms, and only one desk, with no one in view to occupy it.

"You've got it figured. I'm Dan Dunn, and this is my office, and I work without so much as a typist to help out. But it's not all that bad. All I really need is old Ollie here, and I can get the job done."

I shook Dunn's hand and looked at "Old Ollie" more closely. Turns out he was a state-of-the-art personal computer, and Dunn confirmed that he was linked with all the larger more powerful computers in the Department just a few blocks away. This enabled him to access vast data banks, select what he wanted, and massage it to yield insights into any project in which he had an interest. Currently that project was an analysis of all murders in which the weapon was an item of sports equipment, and at B.B.'s request he was zeroing in on acts of violence perpetrated with golf clubs.

"Mr. Trebor," young Dunn explained, "the benefit of a computer in this situation is that it can take a huge amount of input and grind it out in whatever fashion we specify. For example, we'll ask Old Ollie to give us a reading on why one particular implement is used to commit a crime if a number are readily available."

I waited while Dunn typed some incomprehensible instructions to Ollie. After a few seconds he came through.

"See," said Dan with an air of satisfaction, "the overriding reason for weapon selection is proximity. In other words, the assailant grabs the first thing he can get his hands on. But that is true mostly in cases of sudden unpremeditated violence, as the next tabulation shows. Of course we would expect that. But how about situations where the perpetrator has a little time to make a choice? The next tabulation shows that his first priority is to opt for the most efficient tool, one which will do maximum damage with least chance of risk to the user. Again, not too surprising. But here is what I thought most interesting, and I hope it will be of some assistance to you and Tolliver."

With that, Dunn punched more instructions into Old Ollie's brain, and grinned at the results on the screen.

"Mr. Trèbor, this shows what happens if an assailant has a choice of effective weapons available, and time to make a decision among them. In such a situation, the overwhelming choice will be the implement with which he is most familiar. So, a baseball player will grab a bat, while a golfer will choose an iron. Of course this doesn't apply to a badminton player because the racquet is not really a deadly weapon."

Dan Dunn continued, "And look at this: this table shows the results of murders with baseball bats when both aluminum and wooden bats were on hand. Murderers who had been successful professional ball players chose wooden bats, while those who had only participated in amateur competition opted for the aluminum ones. In other words, they selected the particular type of bat they were used to handling."

He had my interest, but I couldn't see where it was going to help me. "Mr. Dunn, are you implying that a golf-type murderer would pick a club with a graphite shaft if that is what he played the game with?"

"I seriously doubt that we can push it that far, but I'd guess that a left-handed golfer might use a left-handed club, and a right-hander a right-handed club, if given the chance. I wish we had some data on that for you."

We chatted on for awhile, but Dunn didn't seem to have anything more for me, so I thanked him and headed on back to the Shoreham. Fiona was waiting for me, and seemed eager to know what I had learned that might break the case, and I replied only that he had given me an interesting angle to chew on. I refrained from discussing what he had actually told me, more because it

106

was good policy not to talk to anyone about details of a case, than because I had any qualms about sharing everything with Fiona.

This went over like flat beer.

"Well, Charlie Chan, just inscrutable yourself to death for all I care, but I'm going to go downtown to the Hirschhorn." Then in a more conciliatory voice she added, "How about going with me?"

I'm sure that the Big H is one fine Museum of Modern Art, but when it comes to any kind of picture that seems to have been done accidentally, I have less couth than a right-wing Visigoth.

"Sorry, Honey, but I have the kind of headache that Salvador Dali could paint. I'll lie low here and catch up on some reports I should have already sent to Lt. Tolliver."

I smiled, and she smiled, and with this reciprocal show of affection nailed down, she headed out to the nearby subway station to hop a train to the Museum.

I sat in the room for a long time trying to work out how Dunn's information could help me, and finally had to admit defeat. Suppose the killer we were looking for didn't have a club with him (or her) upon entering the pro shop. Would he (or she) pick out a club with square grooves to do in old Brasher, just because that was the type they normally used on the course? Preposterous. Still, a little nagging voice inside my head kept twitting me about it, and I wished it would either tell me something comprehensible or shut up.

I'd been lying on the bed for about two hours resting my heart and other vital organs, when I was startled out of my sleep by the harsh claxon the Chesapeake & Potomac Telephone Company puts on its phones to make sure nobody ever lets the damn thing ring without answering it. I answered it.

"Mr. Trebor, I'm Ricardo Ramirez of NONO. I need to see you as soon as possible."

"Well, maybe you are, but what the hell is NONO?"

"I thought you knew. It's an acronym for National Organization for Narcotics Obliteration. Everyone in Washington has to have an acronym. I'm surprised Ms. LaMoste didn't mention it to you."

"Ms. LaMoste and I didn't have a whole lot of conversation about the outfit she was with, except that I had been a drug suspect and then I wasn't anymore."

"Yes, very regrettable. But I would greatly appreciate it if you could meet with me for a few minutes early this evening. You name the time and place."

I chewed this over a bit and decided what-the-hell. "OK, make it Billy Martin's in Georgetown. You know where that is?"

"Yes, Mr. Trebor, I do. Right up Wisconsin Ave. from M Street. Will 7:00 be OK?"

"Agreed. How will I recognize you?" I asked facetiously, almost hoping he would suggest a secret handshake or an elaborate code.

That drew a chuckle from the other end of the wire. "Ah, Trebor, I look exactly like any other wetback in a $500 Brooks Brothers suit."

The honors, I think, went to him.

I took a shower, and dressed as one should to go out in the evening in Our Nation's Capital, although it is always a sacrifice to have to put on a white shirt and tie. I sat around awhile waiting for Fiona to return, and became just a trifle uneasy when she didn't show by 6:30. But she had been looking after herself for a long time, and I reckoned she could do so a little longer without me getting all uptight. Anyway, it was time to go, so I left her a brief note, only saying that I should be back by 8:30 or 9:00, and she should have dinner without me. Then I headed down to the lobby to have the doorman hail a cab for me.

I had decided not to drive down myself, because I hated to leave the Hup parked there in Georgetown. While the Kennedy clan may have precipitated a vast upscaling of the Georgetown area, there were still plenty of unsavories around to vandalize or steal classic cars parked in vulnerable places by foolish owners.

The cabbie dropped me in front of Billy Martin's promptly at 7:00, without whining, pontificating or groveling for a large tip. For this I overcompensated him in the gratuity department, an unnecessary gesture in view of his obvious inability to speak the English language. I walked right in the front door as if I owned the joint, and after my eyes adjusted to the dark, I looked around to see what changes may have taken place in the years since I had last visited.

Billy Martin was an old-time barkeep who ran this modest neighborhood bar on semi-rundown Wisconsin Avenue in mostly rundown Georgetown before Camelot took over the area. He seems to have been smart enough and maybe lucky enough to have moved with the flow, and now had a very respectable establishment whose clientele included a fair number of the affluent. It's said that his son, also Billy, was educated at Georgetown U just to lend the place a touch of class, but I can't verify that. I can verify that the ambiance was comfortable, the seat the same, and the Wild Turkey I ordered smooth enough to complement both.

I hadn't had too many minutes to mull all this over before I felt a tap on my shoulder and looked up into the handsome Hispanic features of the gentleman who called himself Ricardo Ramirez. It was true, as he had said on the phone, that he wore Brooks Brothers suits, but he was about as much of a wetback as Lady Astor.

"Nice of you to come, Mr. Trebor," he said smoothly as he sat down and ordered (honest) a Perrier. "There is a matter the bureau needs to straighten out with you."

If I was supposed to jump off the stool nervously and cry "What is it? What is it?" I missed my cue. I figured whatever it was we needed to straighten out didn't promise instant wealth for yours truly, so I'd let him figure out how he was going to pursue it. I could see the gears working in his head, and as they meshed he began his measured explanation.

"Mr. Trebor, we're pretty sure the real drug kingpin was captured in Charleston, and that should get you off the hook. However one of our agents claims to have some evidence linking you to this illegal activity, and has been able to catch the ear of—"

His voice trailed off and he quickly turned his head to the side as if to hide his face from someone in the room.

"Trebor, a person just entered who I don't want to see me, particularly in your company. I'll duck out through the back way, and I'll ask you to stay here for a short while. Could you be so kind as to meet me in a half an hour someplace nearby?"

I didn't answer, again being satisfied to let him work it out. He thought for a minute.

"I don't want to risk another crowded place like this. How about making it the walking path along the old canal just this side of Key Bridge?"

I didn't like that idea at all, and I probably should have told him to stuff it where the sun don't shine, but I was too curious for that. More importantly, I might have a problem clearing my name of drug involvement, because I was certain that old Winchester was the varmint poisoning the well, and he was out to nail my hide to the nearest wall. If I was going to get this thing cleared up, I'd probably have to dance the next cucaracha with Ricardo Ramirez.

"I'll see," I said.

"Thank you Mr. Trebor. A half hour then?" and he was gone.

The long-abandoned Chesapeake and Ohio Canal runs parallel to the Potomac River, and was intended to allow barge traffic to bypass the falls and rapids of the river downstream to the vicinity of Georgetown, from which point the Potomac becomes navigable for the remainder of its course into Chesapeake Bay. When the canal was no longer deemed to be of any use, it was abandoned and allowed to stay that way for many years. In more recent times, it was rediscovered as a potential recreational asset, and a serviceable path was renewed along its bank. It is in continual use by walkers, joggers, and others who pursue the elusive Siren of Eternal Health. Although it is well lit in spots, most people who frequent this path feel it best to do so before the sun sets. Washington is a large city, and hasn't got the most comforting crime statistics in the Nation. A gunshot, stabbing, or blow to the head can quickly undo all the health benefits that might accrue from an exemplary cardiovascular system.

All this was going through my head as I walked down M Street past the Eagle Liquor store to 35th Street. I crossed at the light and headed across the little grassy plot to the steps that led down to the path on the far side of the canal. Earlier in the day I might have encountered joggers, or even a few adventurous souls bent on paddling their canoes or kayaks upriver to the rough water there. Now however, I was about as alone as I ever wanted to be, and I concentrated on maintaining the degree of alertness my Japanese mentor had insisted was as important as the actual physical techniques needed to stay alive in bad company.

I wasn't reassured when I noted that the light just above the steps, as well as the nearest Key Bridge light, had been rendered hors de combat by a rock or a gunshot, or maybe just by the electrical wires being cut. I kicked myself for not having a flashlight. I kicked myself for being so foolish as to come here at all. I was just deciding to get out of there in a hurry, when matters

110

were taken out of my hands. The hands they were in belonged to a very powerful individual who had stepped behind me and was now demonstrating how much a bear hug could get your attention if the right person was demonstrating it. But even as I gasped for breath, a rational part of my being was wondering what kind of assailant would use such an amateurish, ineffectual means of attack. The intended victim, in this case me, had at his disposal three or four countermoves which could have disastrous effect upon the attacker. As I lifted my right foot and brought it down with force on a vulnerable instep, something went terribly wrong. The chief Lama at some remote Tibetan Monastery apparently used my noggin as his gong, and the instrument he employed to strike the hour was considerably heavier than Lionel Hampton's little xylophone hammer. As I was blacking out I had the sensation of falling into some foul stream which unaccountably also bore the faint aroma of Chanel Number 5.

I had wondered how Fiona felt when she regained consciousness in the Las Vegas infirmary. Now I wouldn't have to ask her because I was undergoing the same trauma in a bed at Georgetown University Hospital. The nurse who was now conducting an inquisition beside my bed sheets had the severe visage of one of the nastier popes, but the most melodious voice I've ever heard. As my eyes came into focus I could see a little twinkle in her eye that said she was one of the good guys.

"Tell me your name, please. Tell me your name. Tell me your—"

"Enough already. I'm Clive Trebor, or at least I was."

"Very good," she said, as if I had just earned an "A" in Nuclear Physics, "that matches your chart."

"What a relief. I'd sure hate to change it to keep your records intact."

Undoubtedly I was acting as nasty as a pile of fresh horse droppings, but the big throbbing knot on top of my head wasn't conducive to a Susie Sunshine routine. I acknowledged same, and Nursie smiled. With that we began a useful dialogue in which I supplied the necessary personal data hospitals are so avid to obtain, and she told me all she knew about my arrival in her ward.

What apparently happened was that the police had received an anonymous tip that there was a body lying half in the water of

111

the C&O Canal, had found me there still breathing, and had rushed me to this hospital. By the time the resident on duty had determined that I was going to live, a Ms. Feather had shown up and had me booked into this private room. Even now she was waiting to see me when I came to.

I remembered only up to the point of being coldcocked with a blunt instrument and probably passing out in the canal. I was relieved that Fiona was here, but couldn't imagine how she had known so quickly.

"Please, Miss, can you send her in?"

"Sorry, I'd like to, but I must get the doctor to look you over before you have house guests."

Before I could protest, she was gone in search of the local Dr. Kildare. After an endless ten minute wait the chief resident showed, did a little routine with stethoscope, and pronounced me fit for visitors.

Fiona came bursting in, all tearful and anxious, and we had to hold each other close for long seconds to drive the boogiemen away.

"Dearest, when I heard, I was afraid that Winchester had made good his threat to kill you. That dreadful man must be put behind bars."

I didn't want to argue with that sensible proposition, but I knew we would need a lot more than we had so far to make that stick. I couldn't even be one hundred percent sure myself that he was the villain. And besides, there were at least two assailants, because one of them had been holding me with both hands when I went bye-bye. So instead of following up on that suggestion I decided to take a more useful tack.

"Fiona, I'm so glad you're here. I was even a little worried about you when you didn't get back to the Shoreham earlier this evening. But how did you find out so soon that I was in the hospital?"

She hesitated just a split second before replying, but it was long enough for me to know that what she was about to say was rehearsed. Hell, you can't be as close as we'd been without sensing such things.

"Apparently the police found your hotel room key in your pocket and checked with the front desk at the Shoreham. They called up to the room and gave me the news. I bet that taxi driver has never driven to Georgetown that fast in all his life—anything for an extra twenty dollar bill."

It certainly sounded plausible, and I began to feel sheepish about doubting. We hashed over the evening's happenings, and couldn't make any sense out of it. The only lead we had to follow up on was one Ricardo Ramirez of a hush-hush Government agency called "NONO." If there really was such an organization.

Next morning I was released from the hospital and sent on my way with vague instructions that amounted to "take two aspirin and go to bed." Instead, when we got back to our hotel room I placed a call for Dorothy LaMoste in Savannah. This might have disturbed Fiona if she had known, but she was safely showering and shampooing, and I had just told her I was going to call someone in the Agency. Lady Luck smiled on me and Dorothy answered on the second ring. I gave her a bare-bones account of the previous evening's fun and games and she promised to go right to work on it.

While waiting for Dorothy's call back, I phoned the police precinct who had picked me out of the canal. They had no record of any hotel room key, and had identified me by the cards in my soggy wallet. They were puzzled that there had been nothing stolen, but theorized that the attackers had been scared off by persons unknown. The desk sergeant was polite, but not too interested in what was probably the umpteenth assault of another long day.

I followed up by calling the front desk of the hotel, but could find no record of any call from the police: "We're supposed to record something like that in the Log, Mr. Trebor, but sometimes they get missed. You can check with the night clerk this evening. He may remember."

I wasn't at all reassured by what I'd learned thus far, but decided not to confront Fiona with it at this time. Heck, it wouldn't be exactly startling for stuff like this to fall between the cracks. I ordered up poached eggs, toast and coffee from room service, and we had just finished polishing them off when Dorothy called.

"Clive, I've been with the agency a long time, and have plenty of connections in Washington, so I'm pretty sure I've got the straight scoop for you. First, the good news: you have definitely been cleared of any connection with druggies. Next, the maybe-good news: Winchester has not been to Washington, or at least has not been in contact with anybody there in the office. And, lastly, the puzzling news: there is nobody in the agency with a name or description anything like Ricardo Ramirez. Frankly, Clive, I don't know what to make of this, but if I learn something I'll be in touch. I owe you."

I thanked LaMoste, and hung up more puzzled than ever. Was this about Winchester's revenge, or did somebody want to remove me because they thought I was getting too close to the murderer of Barry Brasher? And then it struck me that it could be Winchester seeking revenge *and* Winchester being the murderer and wanting to shut me up. True, I had nearly ruled him out as a suspect because he had been friendly to Brasher; but friends do have fallings out. And the so-called runaway car incident in Las Vegas which almost snuffed me, and did bodily harm to Fiona, might not have been an accident. With, or more probably without, Dorothy's concurrence, Winchester could have tried to run me down. Certainly the only persons who even knew about the drug agency NONO were Winchester, LaMoste and (I reluctantly told myself) Fiona. If any of them were worried about me having evidence against them in the Brasher death, they had vastly overestimated the progress I'd made thus far. Of the three, it seemed to me that Fiona was the longest shot, because I had told her so little about the drug thing. Further, I felt that Dorothy had been very helpful in all of this, and if she had wanted to shut me up she could have used her gun on me when Winchester was unconscious and Fiona didn't even know where I was. In any event, I was totally confused, and needed to talk with someone who might help. Clearly, Fiona was ruled off the course, for now at least. Suddenly I wanted to get to Savannah as quickly as possible to hash things over with Billy Bob Tolliver.

12.

Next morning we left early enough to avoid the Washington metropolitan area rush hour. That meant we had to be past Fredericksburg by 6:00 AM. We stopped near Richmond for breakfast, and then ground out another four hundred and some miles of endless nervewracking traffic that is I-95. The fact that the thousand or so inane signs announcing how many miles left to South Of The Border are the high point of the trip tells you something about the beauty of this scenic ride.

We were back in Savannah by late afternoon, and only began to unwind as we crossed the causeway to the tranquility of The Soundings. I had proposed that it wouldn't be smart for us to stay together at this time, and was relieved that Fiona readily agreed. She pointed out that the Brasher house, burdened though it was with an overwhelming mortgage, now belonged to her, along with the complete furnishings therein. We stopped at my rented condo first to put the Hup away and transfer to the less noticeable Cadillac. Then we took Fiona over to her house and got her settled in.

Back at the condo, my first act was to call Billy Bob Tolliver and arrange to meet him for a little light supper at Truffles, a casual spot noted for homebaked bread.

The good Lieutenant greeted me with less than his normal warmth, and I wondered if he was upset with my lack of progress or if I had screwed up in some way I didn't know about. B.B. ordered the king-sized prime rib sandwich while I settled for a tuna on homemade wheat bread. While waiting for our order, he filled me in on what had happened on his end of the investigation. It turned out that progress had been very modest indeed, although one puzzling item had just turned up yesterday when he had gone through Brasher's desk. B.B. promised to show it to me after lunch, hoping that I could figure out what it meant.

I supplied some detail to flesh out the reports I had been giving him by phone along the way. Billy Bob couldn't shed any further light on why I'd been attacked in Washington, but only commented that you had to be lucky *not* to be mugged in that town. I concluded my narrative with the explanation Fiona had given as to how she had so quickly learned that I was in the hospital, and I wound up by saying that I had been unable to verify her account.

B.B. sighed. "Clive, old buddy, I've been nervous about Fiona's involvement in this murder for some time, and I'm afraid this latest episode cuts it. You're too close to the number one suspect, and I'm afraid you'll have to get off the case. I'm really sorry."

That explained his coolness when we met today. He thought he might have to take me off the case, and he was uptight about doing it. I couldn't blame him, but I had too much at stake to just give up.

"B.B., how can you say she's the number one suspect, just because she wasn't unhappy when Brasher cashed his chips? Don't forget we've got quite a roster of good folks who shared her view."

"Clive, you know it's more than that. Besides the motive there's the square-grooved clubs she uses, which is the type your consultant in California says were used to do the deed. There's the fact that she knew Brasher was cancelled by a high-lofted golf club, when that was supposed to be known only to the police and yourself. Now there's this false statement she made to you in Washington."

I made an attempt to interrupt, but he waved me off.

"I'm afraid there's more. I had been puzzled about her whereabouts, and thought perhaps she had left Savannah before the murder, and didn't even know about it in time to attend the funeral. Not so. This morning we uncovered a witness who claims to have seen Fiona walking in the vicinity of the Oleander club early on the morning of the crime. He had been riding his bike, and recognized her as he went by. Even waved to her, and she waved to him. No question of mistaken identity, because he was a nearby neighbor of hers who had often talked to her."

"But how could she have gotten into the locked club to lie in wait for him?" I asked, almost in desperation.

"I'm afraid there's no problem there. We found that Brasher had a key issued to him for his duties on that Golf Committee. Apparently he had had several sets of duplicates made, which we found in his desk at home. Fiona could have lifted a key when she was still living with him. Or, alternatively, she might have arranged to meet him there on some pretext or other. I'm really sorry, Clive."

I struggled a little longer, but I knew it was hopeless. I decided to negotiate. "B.B., how about I stay on the case but don't talk to Fiona about it?"

Tolliver smiled. "Nice try, but no."

We went back and forth a few more times, and finally arrived at a mostly unsatisfactory agreement, but one I had to accept. He would assign me specific aspects of the investigation, none of which would involve Fiona.

We shook hands on it, and I could almost see a sizeable weight lifting off his shoulders. Then back to business.

"Clive, while going through Brasher's desk I found this particular item; maybe you can make some sense of it."

It was the manuscript for an article which apparently had been submitted to The Soundinger Humdinger, the local weekly magazine, regarding the hot issue of the moment, the Equity buyout by the members of the Club's assets, which included six golf courses, two tennis complexes, a fitness center, several pools and three club houses with dining facilities. It was written as a parable set in the 18th century, and would have been a little hard for me to understand had I not heard the bar denizens at the Oleander argue the Equity Buyout topic tirelessly and heatedly on several occasions. I had learned that this was a very controversial issue involving the necessity for each member to come up with some cash to prevent the club from falling into the hands of Kuwaiti or Japanese owners who might conceivably turn the residents' Eden into a popular resort for tourists of all stripes. However, some residents objected to the terms of the buyout.

Apparently the editor had declined to publish the article, perhaps because of the controversy, but maybe because its author seemed to be a few apples short of a full-size pie. Obviously written by a madman, it might provide a motive for someone to kill someone else on the opposite side of the issue. This is exactly how it read, and I'm not kidding an ounce:

A PARABLE

"Long ago, a kindly King decided to develop his vast holdings on Slushy Slough, not far from the old Feudal town of Nirvanah. A little village sprang up, and was soon filled with modest cottages of the new inhabitants, humble people such as bonesetters, toothpullers, feather merchants and used cart dealers; but the wealthy aristocracy of plumbers, politicians and pedants preferred to remain in Nirvanah. The villagers were happy with their lot, and were grateful to the King. They particularly appreciated the support that he gave their two favorite sports, maintaining his mumblety-peg courts in top condition for their use, being sure that the mumbleties were always fresh and the pegs sharp; likewise, the vast caber-hurling courses were carefully groomed at all times. After a few years, the kindly King decided to divest himself of the courts and courses, and believed it to be beneficial to both parties to sell to the villagers. But some of the villagers resisted the sale, although certain patriarchs, some of whom may have been in the patriarching game a couple of innings too long, pointed out that the purchase price was only half the cost of a 450SL Elkcart with dual caribous. Whatever the details, we know that the deal was never consummated, and the King, who even at this point was considered kind of kindly, sold out to the firm of Khadafi & Khomeini, who had amassed a fortune selling neatsfoot oil. (Although neats thrive in many parts of the world, their feet are particularly oily in the Middle East.) The new owners of the "amenities" built a large Inn in the town square, attracting a deluge of interesting visitors from the far corners of the world to use the courts and courses. The villagers relished their presence as an educational experience, and watched with great interest as the visitors bought naughty postcards, cotton candy, and black velvet paintings done in quiet good taste. And from places like Chittlin Switch and Razorback came fun-loving visitors who raised the joy-level of mumblety-peg and caber-hurling several notches. On the courts, spirited discussion was no longer inhibited, and a rainbow of colors replaced the drab white or pastel costume of the past. To calm any misgivings about the number of visitors, residents were guaranteed starting times on the caber-courses anytime after 11:00 A.M. Motivated by the wide selection and very reasonable prices of the many vacant houses, some of these visitors bought homes and moved in. The once-drab houses were soon arrayed in bright and shiny colors. To accommodate the increased traffic, footpaths were eliminated and messy old oak trees were felled to allow widening of the roads. This was greatly appreciated by the younger folk who could now race down the wide streets in their pony carts. And living was no longer so restricted; homeowners could work on their damaged oxcarts or fishing skiffs in the convenience of their own front yards. Moreover, the expense and inconvenience of guards and gates were eliminated, so that a resident would often experience a delightful surprise visit from a loving brother-in-law or a helpful insurance purveyor. So progress and prosperity came to Slushy Slough."

My first thought was that I'd sure like to see the results of the author's Rorschach tests. I couldn't make out just where Brasher stood on this issue, but all the underlining and exclamation points he had apparently littered the manuscript with, convinced me that I should investigate his position vis-a-vis the Great Equity buyout.

Back to what was becoming my favorite hangout, the Oleander Club bar. The regulars knew me by now, and had accepted me as one of their own. I skillfully turned the conversation from golf and women to the Equity Buyout. It didn't take long to discover that Barry Brasher was a vocal opponent, and had caused a great deal of trouble for those favoring the proposal. In fact, right at this bar he had engaged in a pushing and shoving match with Granville Greeb, a key man among the proposition's backers. As he strode angrily out of the bar, Greeb had threatened to relieve Barry of his visible signs of masculinity and maybe more. I couldn't stop myself from speculating if this "maybe more" had been consummated right there in the pro shop of the Oleander Club that bleak morning just past. As of now, at least, Mr. Greeb was right up there on the Suspect List. Fortunately, I had already met this gentleman and even played golf with him. It shouldn't arouse any suspicion if I were to set up another game, and perhaps pry a little information out of him. No sooner said than done; we agreed to meet on the tee at 9:00 the next morning.

The night before, I dug up a little information on Greeb, finding that he ran a public relations firm, and was trying to get the developer of The Soundings to hire him. This was just the opportunity I needed. I judged that if I could give him some worthwhile promotional tips, I could work my way into his confidence, and perhaps pick up some valuable clues.

After 12 holes, Granville Greeb was smiling on me like a possum eating fresh robins' eggs. As his opponent the first six holes

I hadn't been able to even find a par, then as his partner my game had caught fire, with two birdies and four pars. No matter what happened the rest of the way in he was going to show a handsome profit for the day. As we stood on the 13th tee waiting for that slow foursome in front of us to crawl out of range, I plunged right in.

"Granny," I said; "Old Buddy," (I slyly added); "You're a very large wheel in a well-oiled machine dedicated to improving the Ambiance here at The Soundings. That's why I'm going to reveal to you some top-secret ideas which will not only revolutionize life here on the island, but will also make you a hero with persons all over the south end of Savannah."

"Go on," he commanded.

I did. "What our community needs at this point in time and space is a refurbishing of our once-impressive image. As a professional PR man, I can do for you in Georgia what I did for Exxon in Alaska . . . well maybe that's not a good example, but you get my drift. I propose a series of brilliant moves which, when taken together, will have a synergistic effect on the minds and hearts of our fellow Georgians."

He hadn't fallen asleep on me, so I continued. "Our first ploy comes under the category of Hard Sell, and is designed to make everyone realize how much of the local economy is dependent upon Soundings spending. We merely place cashiers at the Security gates, and as each resident heads out for Savannah, he exchanges paper money for silver dollars. Within a week the commercial establishments will be awash in silver, and they'll know where it came from. Since Hilton Head is sure to try to imitate this flash of genius, each resident will carry his coins in canvas bags tastefully enscribed with the Soundings logo. Just like Operation Desert Storm, it's designed to get their attention."

I thought I heard The Great Man snicker, but I must have been mistaken. I plunged on. "Then we go to step 2, which is to show what generous and caring people we are. I know we support all the worthy causes and give far more than our share to all the local charities, but not too many people seem to know or care. We need to be more visible; we need a symbol that everyone can see. And I've got it: a flag."

"Everybody and his brother-in-law has a flag!"

120

"But not like this flag. It'll be the biggest American flag in the state, demonstrating our patriotism; and *patriotism* sells these days. It'll be on a tall mast on top of our lovely blue water tower, where it'll be visible for miles around. It will be high enough to force some of those low-flying planes to detour around the South suburbs, earning the gratitude of residents thereabouts."

Granville must have gotten something caught in his throat, causing odd choking noises to emerge, but he motioned for me to continue.

"As a further community service, the flag will be impregnated with indicator solutions which turn color in the presence of acid rain or odorous emanations from natural fertilizer factories. A chartreuse and lavender American flag is not an inspiring sight, and is sure to stir up demands for remedial action from those citizens who don't like to have Old Glory trifled with."

Again Granville had a coughing spell, but I plunged on. "To cap things off, so to speak, we'll install strain-gauges on the flagpole, which will send electronic signals to a small computer below. When a breeze comes up, the linear deformation of the pole will be translated into miles-per-hour wind velocity. In the event of hurricanes threatening, we'll feed these data to the local radio stations, who. . . ."

Greeb interrupted me (rather rudely I thought) and commenced to tee up his ball.

"But you haven't heard the part about spaying all the squirrels. . . ."

Going into his backswing, he spoke though clenched teeth, "Don't call us . . ." and accelerated through the ball as he finished, ". . . we'll call you!"

He hooked it into the lagoon. Twice. The warm Greeb-Trebor friendship, which seemed to be in full flower just ten minutes ago, plunged into the lagoon with that last ill-fated Titleist. It looked like I was going to have to come up with a different approach to deal with Mr. Greeb. After a stiff and unfond farewell on the eighteenth green, I headed back to my condo to plan my next move. I finished my hot shower just in time to answer the phone.

"Clive? Tolliver here. You can forget Granville Greeb. He has an air-tight alibi for the Brasher murder."

"Are you sure? Allegedly air-tight alibis usually don't hold water, to mix a metaphor."

"This one does. From 2:00 to 10:00 A.M. on that particular morning, the upright Mr. Greeb was in the drunk tank at county jail. He later pleaded guilty to DWI. Not only that, but the Soundings developer won't touch him with a ten-foot pole."

"B.B., if I'd known this five hours ago I could have made two hundred bucks. I don't suppose you'd okay that on my expense account?"

His profound silence told me that no-he-would-not.

"So what's my next assignment, boss?"

With a sigh of relief that I was taking this so well, Tolliver replied, "Two things: first, try to shake up the good doctor out there in California to come through for us now, if he's got anything to come through with. It's getting pretty hot around here for homicide investigators who don't have too much progress to show. Secondly, get back on that kookie professor Corkney Clatter. We checked him out and he can't give a real convincing story on what he was doing at the time of the crime."

Having no other choice, I said, "Aye, Aye, Sir," and began to plan out my approach.

13.

My first step was obvious: a call to Phineas Physis in Palm Springs. He answered on the third ring.

"Clive my boy, this is indeed timely. I tried to reach you just an hour ago. We have an interesting development."

Although I loved him like a favorite uncle, right about then I wished he would quit the damned chuckling and let me in on his little secret.

Always the mind reader, Phineas spoke up, "sorry to keep you in suspense with my senile chortling, but my colleague and I are rather proud of this modest finding of ours. Clive, the weapon of destruction was not only a wedge with square grooves, but a LEFT-HANDED wedge with square grooves!" He paused to allow the impact to sink in.

122

The most important impact for me was that it eliminated one of the factors which tended to point the finger of guilt at Fiona. The words of B.B.'s criminologist friend, Dan Dunn, came to mind, 'a left-hander would tend to select a left-handed weapon, if one were available.' Then I realized that I was keeping the good doctor waiting for a reply.

"Phineas, that's remarkable. How did you do it?"

"Well, pinning it down to a wedge required some painstaking measurements. What made it difficult was that a wedge is angled so that when it hits a plane surface, like someone's forehead, first impact is made with the bottom edge of the face. If this club had been swung normally, there probably wouldn't have been any groove marks on the wound to measure. Fortunately, it did leave a half dozen groove marks, from which we were able to make our determinations. Just how the blow was struck in such a fashion is still a subject for fascinating speculation."

He took a long moment to get a couple of deep breaths. By now I realized that Phineas' fragile health made breathing a non-routine matter. I waited with as much patience as I could muster.

He continued, "As to the left-handed business, that was not a matter of science or technology as much as it was one of prejudice." He smiled at my obvious puzzlement.

On cue, I jumped in, "I don't understand."

"The vast majority of golfers are right-handed, indeed most of us have not played with more than two or three southpaws in our entire careers. Naturally, I guess, when you say 'golf clubs' you mean right-handed golf clubs. That's the trap I fell into on this case. I was worried about a dark bruised area on the side of the primary wound caused by the club face. If it had been on the other side, I'm sure I would have identified its origin as the hosel, the neck of the club head that secures it to the shaft. So it was merely a matter of forgetting prejudice and examining the photos with a fresh and open mind. It didn't take me long to realize that a hosel could be on the 'wrong' side if the club was made for portsiders. Detailed examination of the photos with new techniques my colleague has perfected confirmed this."

"Amazing, Phineas, this could sharpen our focus considerably. According to a criminologist I've talked to, this makes it a reasonable bet that the assailant is left-handed. And you've already done me a great favor." I related briefly the fact that Brasher's ex-wife had square-grooved clubs, and this was a factor in making her a suspect in the case.

"I'm glad I could help relieve some of the suspicion. I perceive that she means a lot to you personally."

The man was uncanny. If I ever commit a major crime I hope that whoever interrogates me doesn't have his powers. I'd be behind bars in ten minutes.

I thanked Dr. Physis profusely, and offered him a fee for his help. He'd have none of it, protesting that he had all the money he needed, and he should have paid us for the fun he had. He did have one request: that I should come to see him soon, preferably accompanied by the 'Lady with the Square Grooves.' That was the easiest request I've ever had. I told him it would be honored as soon as this case was solved, and I hung up feeling more optimistic than I had in a long time.

I phoned B.B. Tolliver to give him the news, hoping that I could be put back on the case officially, and that I could resume seeing Fiona on a regular basis. It turned out to be a letdown. He agreed that it was good news, but there were still other factors which didn't look too good for Fiona, important among them the eyewitness account of her walking near the Oleander Club close to the time of the killing.

"Clive, I've been holding back grilling Ms. Feather till now, partly out of respect for your opinion, but mostly because I didn't think it was good strategy at this point. If we don't get a break soon, I'm going to have to do it, and as you know, those things aren't fun and games."

I well knew it. Tolliver was normally one of the gentlest of men, but I have seen him drive strong men to tears when he puts on the full-court press in the interrogation room. I had no illusions that he would be any easier on Fiona.

B.B. continued, "I'm not quite to that point yet. I promise you I'll make a concerted effort to get more information out of that eyewitness, and I'll try to find other clues as to her actions that morning. Also, it may relieve your mind to know that we're putting part-time surveillance on Winchester's pad in case he shows up. I'd sure like to get him in a place where I could ask a few uninterrupted questions. Meanwhile you do your best to zero in on Prof. Clatter."

It was probably all I could expect from Tolliver, so I agreed to get on with the subinvestigation of Corkney Clatter. Obviously I had to be very cautious not to arouse his suspicions lest he clam up, or worse. I headed for my 'Library,' The Oleander bar, to see if I could learn anything from my drinking buddies.

It was about 5:30 when I entered the inner sanctum, and most of the pilgrims were there, trying to forget the slings and arrows of outrageous business which had wounded them that day, over a tall cold one. I was greeted with some warmth, probably traceable to my calculated habit of buying a round every now and then. The topic under heated discussion was the advisability of removing the flag when chipping onto the green, and I could see it wasn't going to be easy to redirect it toward Professor Corkney Clatter. I mean we were talking momentous decisions here. Advocates of flag removal cited Lee Trevino as their champion, while the anti-removal extremists quoted a recent scientific study which had appeared in one of the golfing magazines. Right in the middle were the wafflers who proposed that really smart golfers left the flag in only for downhill chips.

I let things simmer down somewhat and then put a question before the house: "What does Corkney Clatter recommend?"

This precipitated a mixed response, ranging from murmurs of approval, to mild disinterest, through jeers and cat calls, all the way to a rather emphatic expression of disdain from Farnsworth Flutely. I had to remind Flutely that intentional bursts of flatulence, no matter how melodious, could not properly replace a carefully worded rejoinder.

Thus did I bring the conversation around to Prof. Clatter, and the flagstick issue was forgotten. I soon learned that Corkney wasn't going to win any popularity contest with the majority of the assemblage, although he had his supporters.

One who was firmly in his camp was a dried out little guy with a wispy goatee who was always addressed as 'Muscles,' but who had been christened Hinchley Hobb by doting parents at least seventy-five years ago. I latched on to him like he was going to be the next winner of the Florida lottery. As the crowd thinned, I isolated him at the end of the bar, and started a little game, which he wasn't privy to, called "I'll buy the drinks if you'll sing the tune."

This was like candy from a baby because the tune he wanted to sing was all about Corkney Clatter, and that was my favorite just now too. Unfortunately as the time dragged on, and Muscles was drinking away my not-so-petty cash, I was beginning to wonder if I was going to learn anything other than how witty and bright and talented and intellectual and godlike the old Corker was.

Finally, when Muscles paused to take a well-earned breath, I managed to sandwich in a remark to the effect that I sure would like to see the eminent professor again.

"Hey," squeaked Muscles, "I'm giving a little party for some of the Literati tomorrow night, and Corkney will be there. Why don't you join us?"

I didn't have any reason why I shouldn't join them, and thanked him for his kindness. He gave me his address, which was not at The Soundings, but downtown in the Historic District of Savannah. He had purchased and renovated one of the fine old homes just off one of the squares, where he could, as he put it, 'absorb his share of the rich history and cultural heritage of the city.' He had purchased a lot at The Soundings, which enabled him to join the club and occupy a stool at the Oleander bar, where he could absorb at least his share of the elixir of fine old Kentucky.

Having absorbed about all of this I could handle, I looked at my watch and found that Mickey's long arm was half past his shorter one, indicating that I was late for an important appointment. We shook hands and I exited as if I really was late for something other than a TV dinner I'd have to pull out of the freezer when I got back to the condo.

I spent the next day trying to dig up any information that might weigh in Fiona's favor. I was handicapped by having to move surreptitiously, because if Billy Bob Tolliver found me out, I would be ruled off the course for good. His orders had been very clear on that topic. As a result, I didn't make any giant leaps forward toward solving anything, and the only item I did discover didn't make me ecstatic. Turns out that Fiona had been very chummy with one Patterson Pollipp in the past, and been seen in his company again since we returned from Las Vegas. This really

126

made my molars ache. True, I hadn't been seeing her as much as I'd like, but that wasn't my fault, and she should have understood that. If only I could clear her of suspicion in the murder case I was confident I could send brother Pollipp back to wherever he came from.

Looking back on my day's activity wasn't a morale builder, but I resolved to learn something of value about Corkney Clatter at Hinchley Hobb's party.

I hate most parties because there are too many pitfalls to avoid if you're to escape with a whole skin, socially speaking. The first snare was right here before me even as I began to dress. What would a bunch of what Muscles called Literati wear to an affair like this? No use calling Hobb to find out, because the host will always lead you to believe that casual wear will be fine; and when you arrive you find everyone, including the host, in dark suits with sincere ties. Of course, if you decide that a navy blue blazer and tie are in order, the rest of the troops will be sporting aloha shirts with the tails hanging outside the pants. I decided on the old SKULK or LURK maneuver. I put on full regalia at home and drove downtown to the vicinity of the party early. I took up a vantage point behind dense shrubbery and observed the attire of the arriving guests. Looked like the majority were casual, so I dumped my jacket and tie in the car, unbuttoned my shirt collar, and strode in with the assurance of one who knows he's properly dressed for the occasion.

As I entered Hobb's pad, the host was nowhere in sight, and I didn't recognize anybody I knew there in the large foyer. I must have looked like a lost sheep, because this large bony woman with too much makeup came over to take me in tow.

"Dahling," she said, like she was a character actress in an old Hollywood society show, "I suppose you're looking for Hinchley. The deah boy is engaged in pursuit of one of those horrid little blonde things he insists on inviting to his soirees. I cawnt say when he'll come to greet you properly. But never mind. I'm Penelope Prye."

I'd run into her type a hundred times when I had been on the Charity Ball circuit years ago. Probably had been through three or four husbands and collected enough money along the way to engage in worthy causes, and I was her first worthy cause of the evening. Still, I was grateful to have someone to talk to, so I wouldn't stand out like a sore thumb.

"Thank you for greeting me, Ms. Prye. I'm Clive Trebor, and I don't handle parties well. Perhaps you can give me a little guidance," I responded, shamelessly turning on the vaunted Trebor charm.

"You poor dear, of course I'll help you any way I can," her wide smile revealing a set of choppers so perfect that you had to admire the dental lab technician who had molded them. "Now what's your problem with parties?"

"Well Penelope—may I call you Penelope?" (she nodded enthusiastically); "First is the kissing problem."

"The kissing problem?" Her brow knitted with the question, and it took all those tiny facial wrinkles much too long to smooth out after her face relaxed. This gal was a lot older than her makeup was trying to pretend.

"Yes, you know, when you come in a room, you don't know which women you're supposed to greet with a kiss. I guess I won't have to face that problem tonight, though, because I don't seem to know any of the ladies here."

"You know me, Dear Boy," she replied, and proceeded to land a great big very juicy kiss on my horror-stricken features.

At that moment I knew I was going to have to take unusual action to nip this relationship before it budded: "I know that some women do not like to be kissed by casual acquaintances, while others do," I started off, stalling for time while my frantic brain raced to come up with a plan. "How can you decide which is which?"

As she pondered an answer, a strategy formed in my mean little mind: I would make her want to have nothing to do with me; and I knew how to do that!

Before she could formulate her answer, I spoke up. "I can tell you what I've done in the past, and maybe you can help me go on from there."

"Certainly, dearie."

"Well, I knew enough to kiss the hostess, and any other very close friends, as long as I didn't betray any lustful impulses or damage their lipstick or other facial exotica."

"Of course," Penelope replied.

"But I was puzzled as to what to do about other women who were present. It seemed that you were damned if you did and damned if you didn't."

"True," she said, "so what did you do?"

"Well I just asked the hostess to have all those who wanted to be kissed line up on the right and all others on the left."

Penelope gave me a nervous look, and I noticed she wasn't standing quite as close to me as before. Finally she quavered, "How did it work?"

"I guess my fragile psyche wasn't prepared for the precipitous shift to the portside. But I just went on to Plan B."

Penelope edged a little further away from me, but summoned enough nerve to ask. "What was Plan B?"

"It was really elegant in its simplicity. At the moment of truth I feigned stumbling on the rug, hoping to divert everyone's attention to concern for my safety."

"I see," she said, meaning that the only thing she saw was some kook she wanted to get away from fast. "Mr. Trebor, it's been . . . ah . . . interesting talking to you."

Having solved that little social problem, I began to mingle in the happy throng, and with libation in hand, I began to relax. Serious Mistake. About that time I started running into a series of familiar faces without names. I mean, my miserable little mind couldn't put *any* kind of name on these folks, although I was sure I had met them very recently at the Oleander Club or on the golf course or somewhere. So I resorted to a tactic countless mindless idiots before me have used; "Hi, there!" Well, the target of this sparkling repartee, who immediately remembered who I was, was not named "There," and he was on to my little ploy. I once tried this on a very familiar face at a party, and he replied in disgust, "Come off it, Clive, I'm your father."

There is a better way to remember names, but it has to be implemented when you first meet folks, and it was too late to help me on this occasion. Anyway, the method is called Word Association, and every guru in town is collecting large bucks for teaching this new and wondrous technique, although it is actually quite old. My father used it very effectively for years to surprise and please my mother's many friends by calling each one by name. (The unpleasantness he got into with a certain group of them, whose last names quite coincidentally were Wrenn, Sparrow, Parrot, and Byrd, was an indictment neither of him nor the method.)

About this time I spotted a face and name I did remember: the eminent Professor Corkney Clatter. He was surrounded by a small group of sycophants, each trying to outdo the other in supporting Clatter in whatever discussion was going on. Apparently the rules of the game were that he with the brownest nose won the cut-glass tricycle.

But then Corkney switched the conversation to what he called a philosophical puzzle.

"Gentlemen," he said, "if you observe a coin being flipped five times, and each time it comes up HEADS, what outcome do you predict for the sixth toss?"

There was a nervous undercurrent of discussion, as each loyal follower tried to be sure of ending up on Corkney's side, but no one spoke up.

The professor forced the issue. "How many say that it is most likely to come up TAILS, because that result is long overdue, considering the Law of Averages?"

That business of the Law of Averages sounded pretty good, and a few hands went boldly up.

Clatter deflated them. "Of course that's wrong. We all know that the previous five tosses have no bearing on the sixth toss. How many would agree that the odds are still 50:50 for HEADS or TAILS?"

The rest of the hands went up amid an undercurrent of self congratulation for having thought this out so clearly.

Corkney smiled. "That's very interesting, but if I were asked, I would place my bet on HEADS coming up again."

He paused for effect, and one brave soul couldn't resist piping up, "Corkney, why would you do that? Certainly the odds would be the same for either HEADS or TAILS!"

The Great One magnanimously explained, "That would be true in a perfectly random situation; but we don't know for sure if this is a totally random situation. For example, maybe the coin is slightly unbalanced, or maybe the tosser is in a rhythm that produces exactly the same number of revolutions in the air, or whatever. We don't know. But if unrandomness *is* present, the evidence so far points to it favoring *heads*.

With that, the coterie began to dwindle, probably because no one wanted to be embarrassed again. I had to admire the show Corkney had put on. Not only had he played the crowd like a pipe organ, but he had demonstrated some capacity for deductive reasoning. In spite of his flamboyance, he very likely had enough shrewdness to cause us mischief if he was in the enemy camp. With a certain amount of trepidation, I pasted a smile on my face and walked over to join him.

"Corkney, what a pleasant surprise to see you again. Last time you gave me some instruction on the misuse of cliches, and it has helped my writing considerably."

He grasped my outstretched hand in a hearty handclasp, smiled broadly, and said something to me in a low voice. To bystanders ten feet away, we exhibited all signs of two friends greeting each other.

But what he said belied his smile: "Don't give me that crap, Trebor. You're no writer and we both know it. You've been snooping around asking a lot of questions and I don't like it a damn bit. If you think you can pin something on me just because I said I hated Brasher's guts, you've got another think coming." He accented this last sentence with a powerful squeeze of his huge paw, causing more than a little discomfort in my own slender hand. "What is your game, Trebor?"

Nothing in Clatter's impressive erudition equipped him for what happened next. Apparently he didn't realize that in any handshake, no matter how forceful, the other party's fingers are neutralized, but his thumb is loose to do whatever its owner might ask of it. What I asked of my thumb was merely a little trick my mentor Otsuki had taught me so long ago, which required special exercises to keep the fingers supple and strong, and care to trim the nails to just the right length. The long wiry fingers my genes had provided made it a particularly effective little maneuver.

As Clatter, still smiling blandly, applied more pressure, I responded to his question, "My game at this moment, Corkney, is to keep you from breaking all the bones in my hand." And the ham in me required that I add the old line I'd often heard a stunt man on TV intone, "Do not try this at home. I am a professional."

131

At the same time, I rolled my thumb over, folded its last joint into the back of his hand, and viciously dug the nail in between the first and second metacarpal, causing him to immediately relax his grip and sputter a few words that aren't used in any church I've been to. Now only one of us was smiling.

With an impressive show of willpower, Clatter kept his voice low enough that only I could hear it. "You may find your action ill-advised, you pusillanimous prick. Methinks you won't be doing much more snooping around here." He turned away abruptly, and I lost track of him in the rush which followed the announcement that there was food in the other room.

I should have given it up for a bad job and left, but I was hungry, and no one had thrown me out yet. I freshened my glass of Old Tennis Shoes or whatever and prepared for the Trial of the Balancing Plate. You may know the drill. I was handed a paper plate of mixed comestibles which were either a) low-viscosity liquids, or b) impossible to cut with that polystyrene knife I'd been given. And I was expected to dine on this culinary triumph while perched on a frail antique chair without a table in sight. The first thing I did was to chug-a-lug the whisky before I spilled it on the $80-a-yard carpet. Next, I balanced the plate on my knee and pretended to be enjoying the stimulating conversation. Lady Luck smiled on me, and some other boob spilled his plate on the carpet first, allowing me to escape in the uproar. I scooped the dry edible solids off the plate and into my pocket before seeking out the host to thank him for a stimulating time. I guess I don't understand Literati very well, but the evening wasn't a total loss: I did get to polish off that last drink.

I had parked on the street a couple of blocks away, and as I strode along the deeply-shadowed walk several disquieting thoughts took over my consciousness. The first was the realization that it is almost foolhardy to walk alone on the dark streets of any city at this hour. Secondly, I recalled one of Corkney's admirers relating what a crack shot the professor was with rifle or pistol. Thirdly, I remembered his threat of just an hour ago. Putting together the last two thoughts didn't inspire me to do a Gene Kelly routine around the lamp posts and fire hydrants.

I had almost reached my car when a large forbidding figure materialized from behind the azaleas and planted itself squarely in front of me on the deserted sidewalk. My first thought was that Corkney Clatter wasn't wasting any time seeking revenge, and I might be in trouble. Then I got a better look at the face, and I wished it *was* Corkney, and I knew for sure I was in trouble.

Like one of those nightmares that get worse the second time you have them, Winthrop Winchester crouched on the concrete before me, feet spread, and hands in front as before, but this time one of his hands held a switchblade at the ready. If you want to know what SERIOUS is, SERIOUS is meeting a guy who had almost beaten you unarmed, and now he's back with a truly ugly blade adding about 40% more nasty to someone who had at least his share to start with.

This was one of those rare moments when I wondered if old Otsuki's long-ball training might come up a smidgeon short of clearing the left field fence.

I remember when I was a kid seeing those ads on the back cover of Popular Mechanics, graphically illustrated with this totally ominous character advancing on the hero with large knife in hand. The way he held it aloft so that he could drive it down into his target was absolutely terrifying. The second panel showed the hero, who had completed the mail-order course in Self-Defense for only $19.95 plus postage and handling, bringing his forearm up to smash into the wrist of the villain, causing the weapon to fly harmlessly away.

About now I was wishing that I could duplicate that little trick. The trouble was that Winchester wasn't playing by the rules. As all experienced knife fighters do, he held the knife with the same grip one would use on a letter-opener or paring knife, and he kept it close to his body and protected with his other hand, giving his opponent no chance to dislodge it. W.W. started edging toward me, and I kept edging backward at about the same pace, trying hard to remember everything my mentor had taught me in the lessons on knife-fighting and defenses for same.

His rush wasn't long in coming. As he leapt at me, the blade driving toward my ribs. I stumbled backwards and somehow avoided the deadly knife thrust as his weight slammed into me. As it passed my arm, it nicked my wrist watch, neatly shearing the leather strap in two, but only making a shallow scratch on my arm. It wasn't as miraculous as the old Bible-in-the-pocket-stopping-the-enemy-bullet routine, but I was happy to settle for it.

We both rolled free and were back on our feet facing each other, and nothing had improved a bit. I had this insane thought that if that SOB stomped my watch lying there defenseless on the concrete I'd kill him. I hadn't even had a Plan 'A,' so I had no Plan 'B' to go to. The advantage was entirely his, and he didn't wait around to savor it. Again he surged at me, with knife ready, and I barely was able to deflect the thrust. Then as he smashed his weight into me, something happened that didn't seem to fit the script: the loud crack of a powerful rifle at close range. Almost simultaneously I felt my assailant's body recoil and then go lifeless on top of me, the switchblade still clutched in his hand.

As I pushed his bulk off of me enough to wiggle out from under, I realized there was a great deal of blood on both of us, and none of it was mine. Then I heard some scuffling in the nearby azaleas, followed by vigorous cursing which was noteworthy primarily because it was in Spanish. Pretty soon two uniformed police appeared, escorting a prisoner between them. He wasn't wearing a $500 suit this time, and his military-type fatigues were torn in places, but there was no mistaking the handsome moustachioed features of Ricardo Ramirez.

When he recognized me, his face contorted in disbelief, and he said something in Spanish that may have meant, "Oops, winged the wrong caballero." As I was trying to take all this in, a fourth figure emerged and looked at me with sorrow, "Kee-rist, Cli-uv, cain't you stay out of trouble once?"

14.

Winchester's death had been quick, but messy, and I had been much too close to his body as it graduated to corpse status, to shrug it off as just part of the job. At Tolliver's insistence, I had driven home to my condo at the Soundings, washed down three aspirin with a small hooter of John barleycorn to settle my jangling nerves, and hit the sack for eight good hours of bye-bye.

Next morning a cold shower and two cups of black coffee brought me back to the land of the living. I hopped into the Hup and urged it swiftly through traffic to B.B.'s office to find out what had been learned from the amigo with the high-powered rifle.

It always amazed me how he could look bright-eyed and bushy-tailed after a long night of interrogation and not more than two hours of sleep, but there he was asking me solicitously if I was okay. I told him I was okay enough to listen to him tell me how in the world he and his minions had managed to be at the right place and right time for Trebor's health last night.

"I know you think it was my intuition and genius, Clive," he said, without a trace of the grits-and-grease accent, "but the fact is we got an anonymous phone tip that something was coming down. We haven't been able to find out anything about the tipster so far."

"Well, B.B., I may have that tipster and you to thank for saving my life."

"How do you figure that? Ricardo had already finished off Winthrop, and probably would have vanished without giving you a second thought if we hadn't happened by."

"I don't think so, B.B. When your two uniforms dragged him into the light and he spotted me, I thought his eyes were going to bulge right out of his head. He was absolutely amazed to see me among the living. No sir, I think I was his target, and Winchester got in the way of the bullet that had my name engraved thereon. Remember, it was probably he and Winchester who pulled that same duet on me in Washington."

Tolliver thought this over. "You may be right at that. When we had our little chat with him in the Green Room last night, I had a feeling he was improvising some to explain why he had shot W.W. His story that he had done it because Winchester's drug dealings were a menace to society, was as thin as a three dollar steak. As a matter of fact, we weren't able to break him down last night, but he did give us enough to piece together part of the story. In essence, it appears that Winchester had been turned by the druggies, and was working with Ramirez, who was the Syndicate representative. I think they believed that you were on to their racket, and that the investigation of the Brasher murder was a smoke screen on your part."

"That makes sense," I answered, "Do you think you can get any more out of him?"

My friend smiled, "Is the Pope Catholic?"

It seemed to me that Tolliver had been spending too much time in those big northern cities, because it wasn't like him to bring religion into it.

I began to fill him in on my experience with Corkney Clatter and how he had tried to break my hand with the powerful grip of his good right hand . . . and it suddenly hit me.

"B.B., his right hand was powerful, but he's left-handed! How could I have forgotten! He mentioned it in passing while telling me this long boring golf story the first time we met. Seems to me that takes Fiona off the hotseat to make room for brother Clatter."

"Sorry, Clive. Don't overestimate the importance of that little conversation you had in Washington with Dan Dunn. As I understand it, this only makes it statistically a little more probable that a left-hander like Clatter could have done it. It doesn't prove a thing."

Of course he was right. Why was he always right when it came to squashing my delicate hopes? But at least he acknowledged that it moved the odds a bit in Fiona's favor. Seemed to me right now I should concentrate my efforts on digging up anything I could on Corkney Clatter while Tolliver concentrated on interrogating Ricardo Ramirez, *plus* looking for information that might clear Fiona. B.B. mostly agreed.

"Clive, you be real careful how you snoop around Clatter. We already know he can be a bad apple, and he has threatened you."

My apprehension moved up several levels, because it was not characteristic of Billy Bob to act concerned when it came to the health and well-being of Clive Trebor. He figured I was a big boy, and I hadn't given him any reason to change that opinion in the cases we had worked on together. I'd just have to be a little extra careful how I put together the Corkney Clatter story. With that sobering thought, I left B.B. to prepare for another session with Ramirez in the Green Room, and pointed the nose of the Hup back toward the Soundings.

I remembered that when I first went looking for Professor Clatter I had found him at lunch in the Oleander Club after he had finished a morning round of golf. I had learned that he often followed that same routine, and I figured if I was lucky he would have done so today. I parked the Hup in the lot nearest the pro shop and walked around to the front entrance to the dining room. As I peered cautiously in, I was rewarded by the sight of the Great Man sitting with his back to me at a small table facing the window, undoubtedly boring poor Millie the waitress with another of his patented witticisms. His positioning was fortuitous for me, because he couldn't spot me now, and wouldn't be able to do so two minutes from now when I was inspecting his golf bag and clubs. The only think I needed to worry about was arousing the suspicions of any bystanders thereabouts.

As I walked through the pro shop, I observed that only one person was behind the counter, and she seemed to be totally occupied with deciphering what the computer was trying to tell her about the state of the inventory. Exiting on the far side I spotted Clatter's cart. It had to be his, because his name was printed on the side in larger gold letters than the club covenants allowed, proclaiming to all that this was the property of a very important individual. Nobody else was in the immediate vicinity except the starter in his shack, who seemed to be busy with some sort of schedule or other. He didn't even look up as I walked over to the cart and out of his direct line of sight.

I was tremendously relieved to see that the clubs were indeed made for left-handers. Then I reached in the bag to extract his wedge and give it a good once-over. But there was no pitching wedge there! I checked his implements again from 2-iron to 9-iron plus putter and sand wedge, but still no pitching wedge. Possible, but unusual, for a player of his caliber to carry only one wedge, and that one a sand wedge. While licking my lips at what this was pointing to, I pulled the 9-iron out of the bag to examine it more closely and could hardly believe my eyes. Square grooves. Left-handed clubs with square grooves and the wedge missing.

I conjured up a picture of Corkney Clatter trying to break my hand out of sheer malice, and I said quietly, "Gotcha!"

I couldn't wait to tell B.B. Tolliver what I had found, but it was the kind of news that deserved to be delivered personally, so I headed back to my condo and rang up the station.

Sgt. Rooney answered and told me that 'Investigator Tolliver was not available.'

137

"I've known you too long for that tired old routine, Rooney; can I guess that what you mean is Tolliver has someone's feet to the fire, and won't tear himself away from the entertainment to answer a call from the guy who always saves his old butt for him?"

"Oh come on, Clive," the good sergeant whined, as he recognized my voice, "you know we don't use any form of torture; and certainly not burning somebody's feet."

Of course I knew that, but I also knew that some suspects might actually prefer a little physical foot-burning to the psychological anguish a professional like Tolliver could conjure up. At any rate, I felt a little ashamed for pulling poor Rooney's chain, because he was a good cop even if he probably wouldn't win the Nobel prize in Nuclear Physics.

"Sorry Mike, that was just a figure of speech. Would you ask B.B. to give me a call when he's finished with interrogation? I'd appreciate it."

"Sure, Clive," and I knew he would.

I polished off a toasted cheese on white and a cold Heineken's while waiting for Tolliver to call. I'd heard that time was money, so in view of my lack of any of the real coin of the realm, I decided not to waste its equivalent. I sat down at my breakfast table with a felt pen and a sheet of paper to upgrade our list of suspects:

FREDDY FLATBELLY—Had the opportunity, but apparently not the motive. Long shot only.

GRANVILLE GREEB—Had motive, but seemingly air-tight alibi. Practically eliminated from consideration.

KELLY HERTZ—Had motive, physically capable, will have to check with Tolliver on what his men have found out about him.

DOROTHY LaMOSTE—Had motive, may have had the opportunity. Her position as undercover agent explains some of her actions, but still could have done it. Once a hot suspect, now only lukewarm.

WINTHROP WINCHESTER (Since Deceased)—Motive doubtful, but possible. Disposition toward violence. Still a very long shot.

PROF. CORKNEY CLATTER—Had motive. Exhibits vengeful and violent attitude. Weapon used was one which uniquely fits his possible modus operandi. No strong alibi established as yet. Absolutely the prime suspect at this point.

FIONA FEATHER—Had perhaps the strongest motive. Placed by a witness near scene of crime. Seemed to have information that only murderer and Police would know. Second only to Clatter as a suspect.

As I wrote the last entry I saw with dismay that I had been deluding myself that Fiona was in the clear. The cold facts on a sheet of white paper made even so prejudiced an observer as I realize that she had a lot to explain. If only we could find conclusive evidence that Clatter was the perpetrator. We would. I knew we would.

In the midst of this self-flagellation routine the phone rang.

"Tolliver here. Clive, I got some information out of our friend from south of the border, and we ought to go over it. How about we try that new place over on Mall Boulevard? I hear they have good ribs."

Since the thought of barbecued ribs had him salivating, I decided to hold anything I had to say till later. "Sure, B.B., I can't wait to see what kind of a peanut butter sandwich the chef can create. Six o'clock okay?"

Billy Bob disapproved of my eating habits and didn't know for sure if I was kidding him about the peanut butter sandwich, but he agreed to six o'clock.

I got to Damon's at two minutes past the hour, but B.B. was already seated by the window drinking black coffee and scarfing up the crackers from the little basket on the table. The thought hit me that the management was smart to have those crackers readily available to keep the strong teeth of the Law from eating the napkins and probably the drapes.

I sat down, greeted my friend, and asked him about the results of the interrogation of Ramirez.

"Everything in it's own time, Clive, I can't concentrate on an empty stomach."

"Of course," I said, "I apologize for my total lack of sensitivity in so grave a matter, sir."

If Tolliver detected a note of sarcasm in my reply, he gave no sign of it, as he was busy signaling the waiter to bring over a menu. I ordered a Heineken's and looked over the day's specials for something reasonable to order, knowing that I wasn't going to follow B.B.'s lead, whatever it would be. What it turned out to be was a double order of ribs, potatoes, and a side order of black-eyed peas, which he intended to wash down with more black coffee. I countered with the dieter's special, a sensible portion of very lean ground beef sensibly accompanied by a sensible peach half and likewise cottage cheese.

My gourmand companion grumbled, "Clive, when are you going to learn to eat like a man, and quit all those wimpy foods?"

"Probably never. You know what Shakespeare said, 'Once a wimp, always a wimp.' "

"I'd like to see you sell that to some of the hard cases you've run afoul of since I've known you. Like the late W. Winchester. I'd guess that if Ramirez's bullet hadn't permanently canceled his breathing permit, you would have done the same with your bare hands back there on the sidewalk last night."

Then realizing that what he had just said came dangerously close to being a compliment, Billy Bob added, "Anyway, Shakespeare never said that."

I wasn't going to touch that one. I'd never yet gotten the best of him in quoting Shakespeare. Instead, I sipped on my beer, and when our meals came there was no point in further conversation with B.B. until he was finished.

Tolliver pried the last tasty bit of beef from between his fillings, and pronounced himself well enough to talk about this little homicide case we were on.

"Well Clive, we were right about the shooting last night. After four or five hours under the lights, our boy decided to cooperate. He told us everything we wanted to know about the drug operation, and a hell of a lot more."

"What about the shooting? Was he really after me?"

"Right as two rabbits. He and Winchester were convinced you were closing in on them, and there was only one way to stop you. The script called for W.W. to do it quick and dirty with the knife. When your defense maneuvering made it clear it was not going to work that way, Ramirez panicked and let go a round at your midsection. Winchester's sudden lunge brought him into the path of the bullet."

"What about the anonymous tip?"

"He couldn't say for sure who it was, but wasn't surprised it had happened. There are two factions in the Syndicate battling for supremacy, and he reckoned that one of his enemies was hoping to have the police remove him and Winchester from the playing field. Looks like it worked."

"Did he say anything that would take Winchester's name off the list of suspects in the Brasher killing?"

"Better than that. At the time of Brasher's swan song, Winchester *and* Dorothy LaMoste were in Washington for an emergency meeting. As soon as I heard this, I had our boys contact the Narcs headquarters in Washington. They confirmed this beyond a doubt."

I had mixed emotions about this revelation. I was glad professionally that we had made some progress by narrowing down the suspect list, but that was offset ten times over by the thought that the odds on Fiona had been increased significantly.

Tolliver read my thoughts, "Clive, the time is overdue for bringing Ms. Feather in for formal questioning. You know I wasn't satisfied with the preliminary interview I had with her when you brought her back from Las Vegas."

"Just what didn't you like about what she said?" I asked defensively.

"Come off it, Clive. She was very vague about her whereabouts at the time of the killing. Said she couldn't remember. I probably should have conducted an interrogation before this, but had hoped that we'd learn more by letting things develop. Now we seem to be down to her and Professor Clatter, and maybe persons unknown."

"But what about Kelly Hertz?"

"Clive, I thought I'd told you. It took one of our uniforms only ten minutes to rule Hertz out completely."

"How could that be," I cried desperately, "I spent some time with him and found out that he not only had a motive, but also the physical equipment to do the job!"

"Not quite all the physical equipment," he answered softly, "You see, Mr. Hertz is totally blind. Our man saw him leave his office tapping his white cane. A phone call to his secretary verified this. From what you say, he could conceivably have killed someone on his home territory, but certainly could not have gotten to the Soundings and whopped Brasher in the pro shop."

Seeing the anguish on my face, he continued, "I know what

Fiona means to you, and I promise you we'll be gentle with her as long as we're getting straight answers. Heck Clive, she'll probably clear herself with a few honest answers to our questions; at least we'll proceed on that assumption."

I knew he was doing the right thing, and was bending over backwards to handle it with sensitivity. I also was pretty sure that he would get the answers one way or another, and if she was cleared, it would take a few tons of weight off my shoulders.

"When are you going to call her in?"

"I already have. She agreed to come in at nine tomorrow morning. Meanwhile, it's up to you to keep after the Corkney Clatter investigation."

That shows how our emotions tie us up. In my anxiety about Fiona's upcoming questioning I had forgotten the news I had about Clatter's choice of golf tools. My spirits revived somewhat as I related what I had found.

". . . and when you put together left-handed clubs with square grooves with a missing wedge, he's got to be the overwhelming suspect," I concluded.

"Good work," he replied, without commenting on my conclusion, "Keep after it."

He agreed to call me next day after he had finished talking with Fiona, picked up the check and headed back to his office to prepare his line of questioning. There didn't seem to be anything left for me to do except head back to the condo and try out some positive thinking.

I decided that the best way to keep those unpleasant thoughts at bay was to concentrate on some puzzling aspects of the case. My mind came back to the scene of the crime, and the physical layout of the pro shop. In my mental spreadsheet I listed some of the items I was uncomfortable with:

1) The confined quarters that Barry had occupied when he had apparently been done in. It seemed there was hardly enough room for the assailant to do his (or her) dirty work there.

2) The glass display case wasn't broken, and to avoid doing so the killer would have had to deliver a blow from an awkward angle.

3) The scuff marks on the carpet made by the victim's unspiked

142

street shoes were pronounced, but there were no unusual marks where the assailant would have had to stand.

4) A wedge face forms a sharp angle with its shaft, and for it to make the imprint found on the victim's head would have required an unusual blow indeed.

5) The victim could have broken his wrist when he fell to the floor, but the severe dislocation of the joint and the multiple bone-breaks made this seem unlikely.

The beginning of a thought began teasing the back of my mind, but I couldn't coax it out to where I could examine it. I decided to head for the Oleander pro shop to see if there was anything there which we might have missed.

My calculated habit of buttering up the locals paid off. Mary Alice Nobley was on duty behind the desk, and I had taken considerable pains to win her friendship in the past.

Her eyes lit up as I came through the pro shop door. Apparently she hadn't forgotten that I'd given her a ride all the way downtown one evening when her ancient Chevy had died on her.

"Mr. Trebor," she smiled, "what brings you into our humble sweat shop?"

"Mary Alice," I bantered, "it's only to see your gorgeous face, as you well know."

Miss Mobley was probably about as ugly as the law allowed, and her body might have been presentable if there were eighty pounds less of it, but that didn't stop her from taking pleasure in my flattery. The delighted look on her blushing face told me that Mary Alice would help me out any way she could. Since she was responsible for stock inventories and the like, that might be a good place to start.

"M.A., did you ever get that rotten computer to quit acting up?"

She snorted. "It wasn't the computer, Mr. Trebor, but some of the idiots around here who trifle with it."

"Isn't that always the way," I offered, conveniently forgetting that I had just called the computer 'rotten.'

"Yes," she went on in a rush, "and not only do they mess with the office equipment, but half the time they fail to make a record of stock coming in or going out. Then they blame me when the inventories don't check out."

I nodded in sympathy. "Yeah, seems to me I heard something

about a wedge being missing from the catch-all barrel over there."

"That's a good example, Mr. Trebor, that was another case of people not bothering to write down things they should. But I got that one straightened out." She paused for the expected compliment.

I didn't fail her. "I knew you would, Mary Alice. What was the problem?"

"Well, Professor Clatter had broken his wedge . . ." she trailed off as I broke into a violent coughing spell. "You OK, Mr. Trebor?"

"I'm fine, Mary Alice; just something caught in my windpipe, I guess. Go on with what you were saying."

"Well, if you're sure you're OK. The professor had broken his wedge and we had ordered a new one from the factory. When it came in that idiot stockboy put it in the barrel there with the miscellaneous odd clubs. Not knowing this at the time, I had taken a physical inventory at month's end and recorded the contents of the barrel. Of course the figure I recorded was one higher than it should have been, because I counted Prof Clatter's wedge, which wasn't inventory stock at all."

This time I avoided any sign of emotion, and asked casually, "You took inventory on the 31st, did you?"

"Yes, just two days before that horrible murder." She shuddered at the thought of what had happened right in this room we were now occupying.

"That was terrible, wasn't it? But to get back to more pleasant things, how did you get the inventory thing straightened out?"

"Well, the stockboy was on vacation for a couple of weeks, and when he came back Freddy Flatbelly asked him if Prof Clatter's wedge had come in. The dumb kid finally remembered putting it in the barrel there, but he couldn't remember whether or not he had notified the Professor. Freddy and I looked in the barrel, and it was gone, so we knew the Professor had picked it up."

Yes, thought I, he had indeed picked it up, but when and for what purpose you can't even guess, dear Mary Alice.

15.

I headed back to my condo to do some constructive thinking about this latest development. Instead, I found myself wallowing in destructive brooding about B.B.'s upcoming interrogation of Fiona. As pleased as I was to be strengthening the case against Corkney Clatter, I knew that Fiona wasn't in the clear. I couldn't wait for Tolliver to finish his questioning. One minute I'd be assuring myself that he'd find her absolutely free and clear, then I'd start thinking about some of the disturbing factors B.B. had brought up, and I'd be back in the pits of gloom. The only thing I was reasonably sure of was that he would find out the truth.

I thought of calling him with my latest information on the Professor, but decided against it. I would wait until Billy Bob called me tomorrow after the interrogation. If things went badly I would at least have something positive to fall back on.

I had a couple of bumps of Kentucky's best in a water tumbler, and nibbled at a rapidly cooling TV dinner I'd microwaved the hell out of. Something vaguely disturbing about the murder scene was crawling around in the back of my consciousness and wouldn't leave me alone, but I couldn't quite identify what it was. About midnight I decided I would just have to go back to that pro shop and see if I might be able to solve my problem by osmosis. With that resolved, I fell into an uneasy slumber.

Next morning I arose to see the rain pelting down outside my bedroom, and the leaden sky promised that it was probably going to persist for awhile. Not the best kind of weather for making daisy chains or dancing barefoot through the park. Hell, I told myself irritably, it wasn't the best kind of weather for doing any frigging thing. A couple of very hot cups of black coffee and a stale bagel without lox made me feel marginally better, and I resolved to do some major league deducing. It was either that or slog through the rain to the pro shop and wait for the Muse of Obtuse Clues to strike me with an inspiration. That business of deriving instant revelation by osmosis which had seemed so logical last night didn't hit on all cylinders this grey morning. Like the boys on Madison Avenue would say, I ran it up the flagpole and nobody saluted. So I just settled in and drank more coffee and hoped that that SOB Tolliver would call me before I was eligible for Social Security.

Finally, about three in the afternoon the phone rang once, and I got to it before it had a chance to do a repeat performance. It wasn't Tolliver, but it was indeed the Gendarmes, in the person of Sgt. Rooney.

"Clive, this is Mike. Tolliver asked me to call. He got an emergency summons from the powers that be to review important police business, and he can't get together with you this afternoon."

My reply informed Rooney just where Investigator Tolliver could go, that he could take "the powers that be" with him, and that they could jointly and collectively put important police business where the sun don't shine.

Rooney's normally warm manner suddenly was festooned with icicles. "Mr. Trebor, a police officer is not required to take abuse from anyone. I have a message from Lt. Tolliver, if you care to calm down enough to listen to it."

I certainly did care to calm down. I was too mortified to do anything else. It was totally out of character for me to make such a boorish attack on a nice guy like Rooney.

"God, I'm sorry, Mike. That was really uncalled for on my part. I've been so uptight about his interrogation of Ms. Feather that I guess I just blew my top."

Instantly the old Rooney was back in control. "That's OK, Clive. I understand. The message B.B. left was that he had concluded the interrogation of Ms. Feather."

"How did it come out, Mike, do you have any idea?" I asked desperately.

"I can't say, Clive. But he did leave an envelope for you, and I suspect it may have the information you're looking for. Do you want to pick it up, or should we send it out to you later?"

I assured Rooney that I would pick it up right away, hung up the phone and was in the old Hup tooling across the rainsoaked causeway before Mike had time to finish his cup of lukewarm vending machine coffee.

Sgt. Rooney handed me the envelope and said I could use Tolliver's office, which I did.

I settled in B.B.'s comfortable chair and began reading, my nerves stretched as tight as one of those little strings at the small end of a concert harp:

146

Q: Miss Feather, the last time we talked, you couldn't remember where you were on the morning of the death of your former husband, Mr. Barry Brasher; can you remember now?

A: I wish I could, but it just won't come to me. This has been very traumatic for me, and I seem to be confused about everything that happened back then.

Q: You realize that this could be the most important factor in establishing your innocence; we'll come back to it a little later in the hope that some of the other things we talk about will jog your memory.

A: OK, I'll do my best to remember.

Q: When did you learn of Brasher's death, and what was your reaction?

A: I heard about it that same evening when one of my neighbors came over to comfort me, or whatever. I was shocked, of course, and I think I just blanked out of my mind everything that happened that day.

Q: Were you terribly grieved to hear about his death?

A: As a matter of fact I wasn't even sorry. He'd been a real bastard to me in every way.

Q: Then you were glad that he was dead?

A: Not really. Our divorce was final and he was no longer a problem to me.

Q: But didn't you stand to gain from his estate?

A: Lt. Tolliver, that's a very large laugh. He was in debt to everyone, and I was providing everything for myself long before the divorce. I did inherit the house, but it was so tied up in mortgages that I really netted nothing from it. You can check that out with the bank and the County Tax Commissioner.

Q: As a matter of fact, we've already done so, and you're right.

A NUMBER OF QUESTIONS OMITTED AS IRRELEVANT

Q: Ms Feather, you seemed to have information about the murder weapon that only the police were supposed to know. How did you know that the weapon was a "seven-iron or such" as you told Mr. Trebor?

A: Maybe only the police were supposed to know, but half the people at the Soundings knew it within a few hours. I heard it from my next-door neighbor who was a friend of one of the golf shop employees.

A NUMBER OF QUESTIONS OMITTED AS IRRELEVANT

Q: You were able to locate Mr. Trebor in the hospital in Washington almost before he got there. He was skeptical about your explanation later. How did you find him so quickly?

A: It wasn't like I told Clive at all. I'm afraid he didn't believe the story I made up.

Q: Why did you deceive him?

A: If I told him the truth I thought he would worry too much about me in the future.

Q: How's that?

A: I was just coming back to the hotel when I saw him getting into a cab. I was concerned about Winchester's threats, and thought Clive might be in danger. I followed him to the bar in Georgetown and waited around until he left on foot. I tried to follow him, but he was being very cautious, and I lost sight of him somewhere down M Street. I began to look around the area to catch his trail. Next I heard the police sirens, and followed them to the path by the canal. I got there in time to recognize Clive being put into the ambulance.

A NUMBER OF QUESTIONS OMITTED AS IRRELEVANT

Q: We have talked about your current means of livelihood. It would seem to me to be difficult to continue this . . . profession . . . indefinitely. Do you have other plans for the future?

A: Yes I have. I was always interested in interior decorating, and I've had a bit of experience here and there, and seem to have a knack for it. I've been getting instruction from a friend of mine who is very gifted.

Q: What's your instructor's name?

A: He's Patterson Pollipp, and he has a studio in his home as well as larger quarters downtown. He gives individual and group classes both places.

Q: Where is his home?

A: He's on Admiral Benbow Lane, just the other side of the Oleander Club from the condo I was living in after divorcing Barry. I could walk to his place in good weather.

Q: What do . . .

A: Lt. Tolliver! I've got it! I know where I was that morning: I was at class at Patterson's house!

Q: Are you sure?

A: Oh yes. I walked there because it was a nice morning.

Q: Was this a private lesson?

A: No, there were at least five others there. I'll bet they can confirm this.

ADDITIONAL QUESTIONS OMITTED AS IRRELEVANT

In the margin Tolliver had penciled a note to me: "Clive, I have assigned a detective to check this out with these potential witnesses."

You might think that I would have leapt into the air and shouted 'Excelsior!' or 'Eureka!' or even 'Banzai!', but I just sat their and slumped as all the tension drained out of my overwrought bod. The relief was almost overpowering, and tempered only slightly by the possibility that the corroborating witnesses might not corroborate. But that was a very slight possibility, and I felt I was entitled to ignore it.

As if to validate my premise, there was a knock on the door and Detective Wilson stepped in. We knew each other only slightly, but well enough to shake hands and mutter the usual amenities.

"Mr. Trebor, Billy Bob said I was to deliver this information to you." He paused as I hung on his every syllable.

"I checked out Ms. Feather's alibi and she's clean. I got a statement from Mr. Pollipp and three of his students attesting to her presence at the time in question."

Life can be beautiful when the good guys win a close one. I thanked Wilson and headed out the door, waving to Sgt. Rooney as I left. Tolliver couldn't possibly object to my seeing Fiona now.

149

The rain which had wrapped the whole universe in gloom all day had disappeared, and the late afternoon sun now bathed the west marsh in golden hues as I sped across the causeway for the sanctuary of the island. In a more perfect world this would be the time for Judy Garland to come dancing through the marsh grass singing 'Somewhere Over the Rainbow,' but I settled for the hand that had been dealt me: it was more than sufficient. In twenty five minutes I was back at my condo and on the phone to Fiona.

She picked up on the first ring. "Clive, I'm so glad it's you. I was beginning to wonder if I'd ever hear that beautiful baritone again."

I'd never thought of having a beautiful baritone before, but hey, don't argue with a lady. "Fiona, you're off the hook. That Pollipp character and some of the students corroborated your story."

"Yes," she said, "I feel so relieved and at the same time almost drained."

Then her voice took on a livelier tone. "Clive, Patterson is not 'that Pollipp character,' as you refer to him. He's a dear man and a close friend."

That wasn't the most reassuring thing she could have said, and I told her so.

Fiona laughed as if she'd just heard the world's most amusing joke. "Clive dear, he's just a friend."

I made a policy decision that this was no time to push this thing any further. So I gulped a couple of times and decided to accentuate the positive. Time enough later to deal with the negative.

"Fiona, tonight we need to celebrate, and I think we ought to start with dinner at a really good restaurant. I have Forty-Five South in mind."

Instead of the delighted laugh I expected to hear, I was greeted by a heavy silence. I was beginning to think that we'd been disconnected, but then I heard her dead voice reply, "Clive, I'm so sorry. You know I'd love to go with you, but I can't."

There was another pause, and it wasn't the pause that refreshes.

She spoke again: "I've signed up to go to the Interior Design Symposium in Hilton Head, and it starts this evening."

With a feeling of impending disaster I asked, "Who else is going from here?"

She hesitated, "Nearly everyone in my class."

I knew what that meant, but I had to ask anyway, "Does that include His Saintliness, 'dear man and close friend' Pusillanimous Pollipp?"

The answer came in a tone damned near icy enough to freeze the wire. "Of course Patterson will be there; he *is* the instructor you know."

Then she picked up momentum: "Clive, I've had about enough of your attitude. I suppose the only thing that would make you happy would be for me to wear a chastity belt when I'm not with you. Well I don't belong to you and you can just come off your high horse."

The bang of that receiver nearly shattered my ear drum. Why, I asked myself ruefully, do I always end up the heavy when Truth and Virtue are so clearly on my side? I poured a dollop of Kentucky's Finest to brood on, but found no magic in the first couple of sips and dumped the rest in the sink. With all the bad news, there was one tiny bit of good news: I'd just convinced myself that I wasn't an alcoholic.

Next morning I called B.B. and agreed to meet him at his office to go over the status of the investigation. I figured that work was the only way to keep my personal problems in check.

Tolliver filled me in on the interrogation of Fiona and concluded that she could no longer be considered a suspect. I kept silent, figuring that nothing I might add would improve on that, but Billy Bob didn't seem all that ecstatic at this turn of events.

This irritated me no end, and I let him know it. "What in hell is wrong with you, B.B., did you have a secret wish that Fiona would end up as the killer?

He looked at me sorrowfully. "No Clive, you know that's not true. But this leaves us with just one viable suspect, and we don't have enough on him to convince even me of his guilt, much less a grand jury."

Then I broke the news of the further damaging evidence to Corkney Clatter's defense that I had learned from Mary Alice Nobley at the pro shop. "You can see how it happened. Clatter was notified by the stock boy that his new wedge was in. He picked it up the morning of the slaying. He encountered Brasher there, one thing led to another, and he used his own brand new club to finish off old Barry. One down, a golfer might say."

"Yeah, it could have happened that way. If so it wasn't premeditated, and Clatter will get off with a lighter sentence. But he could have picked up the club the previous day; that is, the day after the erroneous inventory count. Then he might have followed Brasher on the fateful morning with intent to kill. That's Murder One."

While I was absorbing this lesson in how our judicial system works, Tolliver went on. "Maybe it's time to bring him in for formal interrogation, although I admit I'm not too optimistic about breaking him. When we talked to him the first time he came across as a pretty hard customer under all that fat and bluster."

I mulled this over. "B.B., I have this feeling that we can learn more from the scene of the crime than we have so far. You know both of us are puzzled with several aspects of this thing."

He considered this for awhile. "Clive, I have to go along with you on this. If we come up empty, we can still put the Professor on the grill. Any ideas on how we should proceed?"

"How about getting me into the pro shop after hours so I can nose around in private? I have this crazy feeling that I might learn something if I'm on the scene when I do my ruminating."

"I'll fix it up. I'll tell the pro that some of my people will be there this evening, and are not to be disturbed. That way we don't blow your cover, or what's left of it."

"Thanks, Partner."

"Well, Clive, sometimes I think you're a crazy bastard, but I've done all right trusting you before, so let's give it another try."

About seven that evening I let myself in with a key Tolliver had given me and began to look over the shop in more detail than I had before. I had brought along the photos taken with the victim still in place, and related them to the scene I was looking at right now.

There was the glass case full of merchandise, unaffected by the violence which apparently had taken place between it and a heavy metal rack upon which slacks and golf shirts were hanging.

Consulting several of the photographs, I could see that things remained nearly as they had been at the time of the murder, except that the inventory of apparel had changed somewhat, as items had been sold and replaced by fresh stock. Not too surprising that the case and the rack had not been moved, considering that both were very heavy. Furthermore, the large rack constructed of heavy-duty steel pipe was securely fastened to the only wall that was large enough to accommodate it.

I was puzzled by one other thing different from what I saw in the photos. There was now a heavy steel pipe about three feet long projecting at right angles from the rack toward the glass case at a height of about four feet from the floor. I studied it more closely, and ascertained what it was for. A potential customer could take out any garments he was interested in and rehang them on this bar for closer examination.

But why didn't the bar show up in the pictures? I looked at the photos closely and . . . 'Aha,' I said to myself, 'the bar is there, but folded back into the rack.' I set the photos down and began to play with the metal bar. Sure enough, it not only folded back into the rack, but was so loosely mounted that it took just a slight push for it to swing out or to fold back in completely. I toyed with it for awhile, and found that I could make the bar swing out or back by merely jostling it back or forth, up or down. It even swung out when I bumped the rack with my bony behind. I couldn't see what this had to do with anything, but stored it in my cluttered mental file.

I examined the carpet in the area, but found only normal footprints in golf spikes and street shoes of people walking and standing. It obviously had been vacuumed several times since the murder, erasing any clues that might have been there. I scanned the photos of the carpet as it had appeared at the scene of the crime. It seemed that a person in street shoes, presumably Brasher, had been standing with his back to the clothing rack, feet spread about eighteen inches apart. Where his left foot had been there was a long scuff mark, as if the foot had been knocked out from under him in the attack. Facing toward Brasher were a number of spiked footprints, at least some of which were probably made by people looking at the clothing. Since there was no evidence of any other prints from street shoes, the assailant must have been wearing golf spikes. I wandered over to the barrel of miscellaneous wedges and putters. It looked the same as the pictures showed. Next to the barrel were two bags of clubs which hadn't shown up in the pictures. Probably meant nothing, but I looked them over anyway. Each bag had a large tag marked STORAGE LOCKER bearing a name and address and today's date. One address was in Connecticut and the other in Illinois. I knew that there were club members who lived in the North and spent only part of the time here, and presumably two of them had left their clubs here today, to be put in storage tomorrow morning when the day crew came on duty.

I spent another half hour nosing around the shop, comparing things now to what they were at the time of the crime, but all I was getting was frustrated. I locked up and headed back to my condo to contemplate my navel, or whatever those Gurus do to discover all truths.

I was just pouring my absolutely first bourbon of the evening when a couple of things started to come together in my cluttered little mind. I suddenly recalled what Dr. Phineas Physis had said about working out a problem sometimes being a matter of looking at things from a non-obvious point of view. Then I thought about what Dan Dunn had said, and a bizarre thought struck me. I set down my glass, untouched, and sorted through the photos until I found one of Barry Brasher's body on the pro shop carpet. 'Bingo,' I said to myself out loud.

The scenario I had just dreamed up was straight out of Edgar Allan Poe, and a crucial piece of the puzzle was still missing. I had a theory on where that piece might be, but it was a very long shot indeed. Well, I thought, why not? Satisfied with that profundity, I rewarded myself with a wee sip from the glass that had magically appeared in my hand.

I was hesitant to go to Billy Bob Tolliver with such a wild unproven theory, but I couldn't see how to pin down the crucial facts without his help. Besides, he had enough experience with my hare-brained ideas in the past to know that a pretty good percentage of them were proven true. 'What the hell,' I told myself, and resolved to call Tolliver in the morning.

Just as I was finishing my drink, the phone rang. I willed it to be Fiona. It wasn't.

"Clive, this is Dorothy LaMoste," the familiar sexy voice intoned.

"Dorothy! I hoped it was Fiona," I blurted out, boorishly putting my size-ten hoof in my mouth.

"Well isn't that a nice way to greet a friendly voice? As a matter of fact I saw Fiona this morning at the show on Hilton Head. She and Patterson Pollipp were staying till this afternoon for the last seminar, but I had to get back here early to handle some business."

I didn't answer right away. Fiona and that Pollipp bastard alone together on Hilton Head, and without even Dorothy LaMoste to chaperone! God I had lost her for good!

"Clive, are you still there? Because if you are I'd like to ask you if it's OK if I stop by and chat a bit. Something that might interest you."

"Of course . . . Dorothy," I stammered, "come on by."

After I hung up, and began to pick up dirty socks and sweep dirt under the rug, it occurred to me that this might be one of the dumber things I'd done in a long number of fortnights. Suppose Dear Dotty was coming by for more of her cookies and milk routine? Suppose Fiona walked in when the two of us were in a compromising situation? Suppose . . .

But what the hell. It was too late now. I should have thought of all this before I said 'Come on by.'

The door bell sounded unnaturally loud, almost making me spill that little bump of Kentucky's best I'd poured for fortification against what might come. I ushered Dotty in, making no move toward kissing her, even on the cheek. It didn't matter. Before I could jump back in horror she had me enfolded in her relentless embrace, her ample breasts against my chest, her soft red lips pressed hard on mine. I was giving a good imitation of the hapless rabbit caught in the coils of the boa constricter when she suddenly drew away with an amused grin on her beautiful face.

"Poor Clive, are you absolutely terrified that Red Hot Mama will steal your virtue?"

I reddened. "Dammit Dorothy, you know how I feel about Fiona."

She sobered. "I do now, dear Clive, but I went into my Cleopatra routine just now to check you out. If you'd reacted like Mark

155

Anthony, you'd have made the top spot on my black list, and Fiona would know about it in no time flat. You see, she and I have become friends in the last few days, and I don't want to see her getting hurt again."

It took me awhile to recover, and all I could think of to say was, "I thought she still hated your guts for your little fling with her then-husband Brasher."

"No, apparently she'd done a lot of thinking about it and realized that I was just a fellow victim of Barry Bastard."

"Did you come over here just to embarrass the hell out of me with that Instant Passion scene?"

"Of course not. What I came for was to get it through your one-track mind that Fiona loves only you, God help her, and you'd better not screw it up with your silly jealousy act."

"Wait a minute, LaMoste; she's seeing this Pollipp character more than she's seeing me, and she keeps telling me how nice he is. I'm not about to start a fan club for the lousy bastard, and I don't think Fiona should either."

"Clive, he *is* a nice guy, but he's just our instructor, nothing more. . . ."

Then a light bulb went on inside Dorothy's perfectly formed skull and lit up her beautiful face. "She didn't tell you, did she? Clive, you lame-brain, Patterson Pollipp is GAY. His interest in Fiona is strictly business."

I guess I'm an old-fashioned type who doesn't understand the Gay Community, and I never thought I would be overjoyed to learn that someone was gay, but right at this moment I enthusiastically supported Mr. Pollipp's sexual persuasion.

Dorothy kissed me on the cheek, murmured something that sounded like 'Verbum Sapienti Satis,' and evacuated the premises. Some day I'm going to look that up in my Latin Dictionary.

Early to bed, early to rise. By eight AM I had showered, shaved, and breakfasted on a Bismark flushed down the old gullet by three cups of Trebor special coffee, brewed in a pot which had never been contaminated by soapy water. I crossed my fingers, called B.B., and told him I had to see him. He agreed to meet me for lunch at the Crystal Beer Parlor downtown. This establishment was reputed by many to serve the best burgers in the civilized world, and you'd get no argument from Lt. Tolliver, who believed that if it was made of beef it had to be good.

I managed to nearly finish my Dieter's Special burger plate in the few minutes it took Billy Bob to polish off two large cheeseburgers with a double order of fries.

He wiped his chin, grinned at me, and said, "Now tell me what has got you in such a dither, Cliv-o. Your fidgeting and squirming has got to mean that I'm about to hear one of the famous Trebor scenarios extraordinaire."

I winced, and he wrung his hands in delight at having struck paydirt. Well at least he was prepared for the worst. I laid out for him my reconstruct of the last day on earth of one Barry Brasher, certified bastard.

"Whooeee, Cli-uv, yo have sho-nuff topped yo'self this time. An' Ah was a-thinkin' it were somethin simple like a big ole hound dawg poppin Brothuh Barry with thet golfin' stick."

I had come to expect Billy Bob to lapse into his grease-and-grits accent when he got excited, but this was too much. He was really rattling my chain, and I was defensive enough to get a little hot under the collar at how he was taking it.

"No one asked you to believe it, sir. I just thought it my duty to bring all pertinent information to my employer," I huffed snottily.

"Slow down, Clive, I couldn't help but react a little strongly. After all, this does put quite a different twist on things." He smiled.

"Sorry, B.B.," I said, "I just didn't want you to brush this off. If you're willing, there's a way we can test my hypothesis further."

"Sure, Clive. It's too damned interesting not to give it a full shot. Tell me what you have in mind for us to do next."

I told him.

That evening about seven I met B.B. and a crime lab technician at the Oleander pro shop. It didn't take long to obtain the samples we needed, and we crossed our fingers that the clue we were after hadn't been erased by time or human activity.

Just before noon next day Tolliver called me. "Clive, the lab boys did a rush job for us and it checks out just the way you figured."

I breathed a sigh of relief, "Good. Now for the hard part. I can't figure this last piece of the puzzle at all, but there must be an answer waiting for us if we know what questions to ask and who can answer them."

"Wish I could help, but I'm in the same boat. Maybe you can do some more snooping around the pro shop. You might run on to something."

Seemed like it was a bloody go, as some of my prep school classmates would have said, and if I stumbled on to a few of the right questions I was sure that my friend Mary Alice Nobley would do her best to answer them.

On the way to the Oleander pro shop I detoured by Savannah Sweets in the Oglethorpe Mall to pick up a generous supply of pralines. I guessed that if there was anything in the world that Mary Alice might go for, it was those little mounds of almost pure brown sugar, lightly caramelized, loaded down with pecans, and ready to ruin your teeth and gums. When I entered the shop and handed her the box of goodies, my judgement was vindicated.

"Oh Mr. Trebor, how did you know I love pralines? Normally I don't like sweets that much, but these are different."

I refrained from reacting, although I thought to myself that I'd hate to be a chocolate bar or peppermint patty alone with Ms. Nobley for half a minute.

Instead, I merely said, "Glad you like them. M.A., I just made a guess that you would when I was taking inventory in my pantry a while ago. Is Freddy Flatbelly around?"

I knew that he wasn't, as I had seen him headed across the causeway just minutes ago, but this way Mary Alice wouldn't question my reason for being there.

She verified that he was gone for the day. "Anything I can do for you, sir?"

I wasn't sure just where to begin, but one thing I did want to check on was those bags tagged for storage I had seen in last night's visit. So I went into my routine.

"Gee, I guess not . . . wait, come to think of it, maybe there is. A friend of mine is planning on spending a couple of weeks here every now and then when he can break away from his ostrich food business in Michigan. He was wondering if he could store a

158

set of clubs here between visits. Being from Detroit, he's very cautious, and wants to be sure they won't be lost or stolen."

Mary Alice giggled in delight. "Mr. Trebor, he can not only store them with us, but he can be sure they won't be lost, strayed or stolen. Like everything else around here, the club storage system in place when I arrived on the scene was really haphazard. Nothing was ever stolen, because our members wouldn't do that, but a lot of foul-ups occurred. Now everything is accounted for at all times," she finished with a verbal pat on her own back for a job well done.

I looked suitably impressed. "How do you manage that?"

"The system is really very simple. Basically we use this log book here behind the counter." She produced the book, and opened it to show how it worked.

"When someone leaves a bag for storage, I mark the name in the first column here, the date in the second column, and the actual time of day in the third. At his very first opportunity, the stock boy picks up this key to the locker, and puts the bag there. He then records the date and exact time in the next two columns, and initials it. When the member comes for his bag later, the stock boy gets it for him, and records the exact time and date in the last columns."

"Sounds good to me. But is it really necessary to record the time of day as well as the date?"

"I know it sounds like overkill, but we have had a stock boy or three from time to time who weren't too careful about when they performed their duties. Like Timmy who's in the job now; not dishonest, just lazy. You'd be surprised how this little discipline works. No one is going to put in a phony time if they know I'm checking on them constantly." Mary Alice leaned back in satisfaction as if she had just discovered a better way to split the atom.

I began to study recent entries in the book which she had just passed over the counter for my inspection and adulation.

"Mary Alice, I note that you checked in two bags at 4:45 PM yesterday, but the stockboy didn't store them away until 7:15 this morning." I was referring to the two bags I had spotted in my visit last night.

"Yes, that does happen. Timmy works from seven in the morning to four in the afternoon. If anything comes in for storage after

159

his shift is over, I just put it over there by that big barrel and keep an eye on it until we lock up. Your friend doesn't have to worry about that."

"My friend? Oh yes, my friend from Detroit," I stammered. I'd almost forgotten that fictitious sonavabitch.

"Look at this, Mary Alice," I said, pointing to an entry a few weeks before. "You checked a bag in for a Mr. Horace Hacker on April 1st at 5:00 PM. The stock boy stored the clubs away next morning at 7:13. Mary Alice, that was the morning Mr. Barry Brasher departed this world!"

"Boy, do I remember that! Timmy came into the shop just after Mr. Flatbelly had discovered the body, and was on the phone to security. Timmy picked up Mr. Hacker's bag and took it to storage and locked it up. He came back into the shop and recorded it in this book as he was trained to do. Only then did he look over to where poor Mr. Brasher lay on the floor . . ." Mary Alice was looking not too 100% at this moment, but she gritted her teeth and went on.

"Timmy could hear Mr. Flatbelly throwing up in the john, and was afraid he was going to do the same. He bolted out the door and didn't stop until he was about three fairways away. By the time he felt composed enough to come back, I'd arrived for work, but the police wouldn't let anyone in. I told Timmy to go home, and he would be paid for the day anyway."

Ms. Nobley didn't seem to notice the expression on my face, as she regrouped. Then, with obvious pride in her voice, she offered, "See, Mr. Trebor, my system works under the most trying circumstances!"

'You bet it does, Honey,' thought I. Aloud I said, "Mary Alice, you can be proud. How about showing me how the clubs are stored, to complete the picture?"

"Sure, Mr. Trebor."

She picked up the key from the desk drawer and led me back to the storage room and unlocked the door. We could see about a dozen bags neatly lined up in a rack along the wall.

"The bags are lined up in the chronological order in which they were received. See, these two here up front were stored just this morning."

"Is Mr. Hacker's bag still here?"

160

"Well it had better be, because it still shows on the book. Yes, there it is about half way back, that oversize red and white Wilson bag."

I restrained myself from going over to touch it, but I eagle-eyed it from where we stood. My heartbeat must have hit about 150 when I spotted what I had been looking for but was afraid wasn't there.

Ms. Nobley didn't notice my agitation. "Mr. Trebor, would you like to look a little closer?"

"No, the way I'm playing these days I wouldn't want to hex any of these guys by touching their bags," I lied, insuring that Mary Alice would be able to testify that I hadn't tampered with anything in that locker.

I bid Ms. Nobley adieu as rapidly as civility would permit and hurried back to my condo to call Lieutenant Tolliver.

He picked up on the second ring. "Tolliver here."

"B.B., the last piece of the puzzle is about to fall into place." I quickly described my visit to the pro shop and; my conversation with Mary Alice Nobley.

"Cli-uv, you' jest won thu cut-glass buggy-whip!" He laughed, and continued in a more normal voice. "And just in time too. My peerless leader, the eminent Capt. Frank 'Icy' Frost has informed me that we have until midnight tomorrow night to clear this up or we all get thrown to the wolves. An old buddy of mine in the Public Relations Department told me a public announcement has already been drawn up detailing a big shakeup in the department. Icy let me know I am to be one of those most grievously shaken up."

"Those totally pompous asses!" I exploded. "Do they think all you have to do is punch a few keys on the computer and a murderer automatically comes popping out? Even with this breakthrough, it's going to be almost impossible to wrap up the case by tomorrow night!"

"Don't go ballistic on me, Clive. What you say is true, if we follow normal systematic procedure." He paused and furrowed his leathery brow. "How confident are you that we've got this thing straight?"

"At least 90% sure."

"Well, I say we go for it. Fast track it, as they say at the FBI."

"Just how do we do that?"

"There's still time this afternoon to send the lab boys out to the pro shop and collect the evidence. By midafternoon tomorrow they should have results of their analyses. Meanwhile we take a deposition from the stock boy, Timmy, in the hope that he can make things a little more plausible. Then tomorrow at five o'clock we throw a party right there in the Oleander pro shop."

"What kind of party, Billy Bob?"

Tolliver chuckled so loudly I could visualize that big belly jiggling like a department store Santa Claus, "There won't be any refreshments, but plenty of entertainment. Kind of like Show-And-Tell, starring Clive Trebor and his magic wand."

"No, Billy Bob, you're in charge of the investigation; you should be the one to do it."

He shook his head. "You came up with the solution, and if it bombs out, you deserve your share of the brickbats."

What he really meant was that if it worked out as we thought it would, I deserved the credit, but he was always too embarrassed to actually compliment anyone, particularly me.

"I presume you've decided on a guest list?"

"Yep, first has got to be my beloved boss, Capt. Frost. Next, the coroner, who could save us a lot of red tape later. I figure we ought to have Claude Cobra, the assistant D.A. who's been whipping up dissatisfaction with the way things have been conducted by yours truly. Last, we invite the three principal suspects, Professor Clatter, Ms. LaMoste and Ms. Feather."

"But B.B., why invite all three of them? You agreed that Dorothy and Fiona were cleared."

"Well Clive, look at it this way. They were under the trauma of suspicion, and deserve to know exactly what did happen. But also, suppose it turns out that we are only partly right as to the ugly events of that morning. It might not be a bad idea to have the right players available for Scenario 'B'."

I could see what he meant. We wouldn't know for sure that we had it right until the lab boys completed their work.

"B.B., can't we wait until we get the lab results before we invite all these distinguished guests?" I was really getting uptight about the thought of having egg on my face in front of these kinds of witnesses.

"Don't I wish. No, we can't have results before midafternoon, and that would be too late to invite these people and get them to show up. But if we don't get the results we expect, we can cancel the whole show at the last minute. That won't win us any fans, but by then we don't have too much to lose."

Done and done. I hung up feeling like a trapeze artist who's about to try a quadruple something-or-other for the first time and somebody has stolen the safety net.

16.

At about 4:35 next afternoon I got a call from Lieut. Tolliver. His usually professional manner was tinged with what sounded suspiciously like the first stages of panic. He had been called out to Statesville that morning, and been delayed more than he had expected. When he got into his police cruiser for the trip back to Savannah the damn car wouldn't start. By the time he'd gotten a local mechanic to look at it, it was nearly three o'clock. He had called his office and left word for the two police lab technicians to meet us at the Oleander Club with their results. Turned out the car was just suffering from vapor-lock and he'd burned rubber back to town.

"Clive, I'm on the way, but it'll be a few minutes after five when I get there. Try to keep the natives from getting too restless."

"Did you find out how the test turned out?"

"Not a clue. We're going to have to cross our legs and hope the fates don't screw us." He hung up.

'Oh this is really great,' thought I, and headed for the pro shop. I hung around outside hoping to spot Foster and Brown from the crime lab before talking to anyone else. About two minutes before five they drove up, and I ran out to the parking lot to intercept them.

I hailed Brown, the senior man, "What were the results of the tests?"

Brown looked embarrassed. "Sorry Mr. Trebor, but we have

strict instructions not to discuss them with anybody except Lieut. Tolliver."

"For God's sake, Brown, I'm working with Tolliver on the investigation, and he's going to be late and . . ."

I broke off in frustration, knowing from the way they were shaking their heads that I was shouting into the wind. I turned and headed back to the shop. As I entered, I could see everyone milling around in front of the folding chairs which had been set up by the desk. The area encompassing the big glass case and the clothing rack had been cordoned off by a yellow rope.

Fiona and Dorothy were standing together in animated conversation, occasionally looking over at me, then turning away when they saw I was looking. Professor Corkney Clatter was sitting in one of the chairs, which didn't seem big enough or strong enough for his impressive bulk. He was scowling a world-class scowl. The coroner, a gaunt dark-skinned man of middle age, stood by himself doing what he was famous for: saying nothing to anybody. Claude Cobra, the Assistant D.A. with the smallest fan club in the police department in recent history, was haranguing Captain Frost in a way that did not promise a fun time for Lieut. Billy Bob Tolliver or his irrepressible sidekick, the intrepid Clive Trebor. Everyone was present except B.B. I was alone in the coliseum, and the lions began to circle me.

I tried to get everyone to sit down and be patient, explaining B.B.'s car problem, but Claude Cobra would have none of it.

The Assistant D.A. give me a contemptuous look. "I'm not going to wait one damn minute more for some wild side show Tolliver has dreamed up."

He turned to Capt. Frost, "Icy, I've told you before you shouldn't put up with any more of his schemes. Maybe he has been lucky a few times, but I say his luck has run out."

This was bad enough, but even worse was the way that bastard Frost nodded in agreement. I never realized before what kind of burden B.B. had to labor under.

"Please sit down, Mr. Cobra," I said in a cheery voice that belied my inner conflict, "I'll begin the presentation and Lieut. Tolliver will be here before I'm done."

He reluctantly eased himself into a chair, mumbling ominous mumbles about the future manning of the police force. The others settled down as well, eager to hear what sort of tale we had to tell.

I related how the investigation began with the first examination of the body lying on the carpet not ten feet from where I was now standing, and brought things almost up to the present.

As I described how we had characterized the weapon of destruction as a left-handed wedge with square grooves, I could see expressions of interest and incredulity. But I was most intent on watching Corkney Clatter. First the color drained from the fleshy features in shock at the implications of what I said. This was followed by the scarlet of gathering rage, and then the purple of indignation.

"It's a frame-up," he hissed.

I continued with an account of our investigation of the various suspects: Dorothy, Fiona, Hertz, Winchester, Greeb. I told how each had been cleared.

Finally I got to Prof. Clatter. I pointed out that he had admitted his hatred of the victim; that he had no alibi for the time of the murder; that he was left-handed and used square-grooved clubs. I watched the rage and hate build in Corkney Clatter as I continued my damning litany.

I decided to confront him directly. "Professor, is it true that your wedge is missing from your bag?"

"You know it is, you sadistic prick!" he bellowed, "but what you may not know is that I broke it months ago and have been waiting for a new one to be delivered."

"Oh, we know that, but we also know that your new wedge was delivered to the pro shop before Brasher was killed."

"You're lying!" he screamed, and almost rose from his chair.

"We'll see," I said. "Officer Brown, let me have it please."

Brown handed me a golf club with a red tag affixed to its shaft.

"Ladies and Gentlemen, this is a new Smedley SquareSmack wedge, registration #32334, made by the manufacturer to match the set of Professor Corkney Clatter."

Clatter jumped out of his seat and launched his huge bulk toward me. Almost simultaneously the door burst open and Billy Bob Tolliver was at Clatter's back, twisting his arm up behind him.

"Yo' bettuh hold yoah hosses, old son, afore some'uns gits hurt," intoned B.B., as Corkney cringed in pain.

Tolliver released his hold on the Professor's arm, and at the same time slammed him down in his chair. He motioned Foster to keep Clatter under control and walked over to confer with Brown. I could see the latter pointing to one another of the sheets of paper he held in his hand, but couldn't hear what he was saying. Then the Lieutenant turned with a broad grin and gave me the thumbs up signal.

I nearly wilted to the floor in relief, and probably would have just slumped in one of the chairs as the tension left me, but Tolliver gave a vigorous "Roll 'em" signal and it was Show Time again.

"As I said, this is not only Professor Clatter's new wedge, but we allege it to be the instrument which killed Barry Brasher."

Clatter had become incoherent in his mumbling, and only subsided completely when Foster applied further pressure to a vulnerable point in his shoulder.

I continued, "I'll ask Officer Brown to step over here. Officer, what did you find on the head of this club when you analyzed it this morning?"

"Two things, sir, microscopic traces of human tissue on the face and leading edge of the club head, and a handprint pretty well covering the entire club head."

"And were you able to identify the human tissue?"

"Yes, sir. Each human being's DNA is unique to him alone, and is found in no other person on earth. The very latest techniques allow us to analyze for this unique tracer in the tiniest amount of tissue."

"And have you identified whose tissue this is?"

"Yes sir. We matched it to Mr. Barry Brasher."

"Very impressive. It appears that this was indeed the weapon that removed Mr. Brasher from this vale of tears. Now about the hand print on the club head, did you identify that?"

"Oh yes, that's very simple. The print was made by one Timmie Trout, the stock boy at this pro shop."

"Fine; we'll get back to that later. Now, moving up the shaft of this club what did you find?"

"It was obviously a new club, because the grip was still wrapped in cellophane for protection. That made it possible to lift finger-prints from the surface."

"What kind of prints did you find?"

"There were several indistinct and fragmentary prints such as might have been acquired in wrapping and handling, but the dominant feature was a set of prints of both hands of an individual gripping the club tightly."

"Thank you. Now, Ladies and Gentlemen, I submit to you that these had to be the prints of the person who struck the death blow!"

There was a murmur of excitement in the room, but no one challenged my statement.

"Officer Brown, I understand that you compared these prints with those of two individuals, who we shall designate as 'A' and 'B'. Did 'A' match these prints?"

"No sir."

"Would you now identify 'A'?"

"That would be Professor Clatter."

In the hubbub that followed, I watched Corkney Clatter. He was like a man who suddenly awakened from a bad dream and couldn't believe that he was really safe from the hobgoblins who had been torturing him. He was laughing and crying at the same time, and kept muttering to no one in particular that they hadn't been able to frame *him*. As he subsided I continued.

"Now, Officer, did the prints from 'B' match the prints on the grip of the club?"

"Yes sir."

That room became so quiet that I swear no one was even breathing. All ears strained to hear the answer to the next obvious question.

"Would you please identify 'B'?"

"Sir, 'B' was Mr. Barry Brasher."

The angry voice of Claude Cobra broke the stunned silence, "What in hell are you guys trying to pull?! Do you expect us to believe that Brasher committed suicide with a golf club? Frost, this is ridiculous. I demand you relieve Tolliver of his duties, and ship this buffoon," (as he pointed to me), "back to the loony bin he came from!"

Capt. Frost surprised me. I doubt that he had any thought of loyalty in mind. Probably he knew from past experience that Tolliver was no dumbbell, and he didn't want to be on the wrong side if this bizarre hypothesis proved to be true. At any rate he spoke up.

"Lieutenant, would you be so kind as to explain what you two are talking about?"

"Yessir," B.B. replied, "But Brasher did not commit suicide. We will show that it was a tragic accident. With your permission, Captain, I'd like for Mr. Trebor to continue."

Frost looked toward me and nodded.

"This is our reconstruction. It may be inaccurate in a detail or two, but we are confident that the gist of it is true. On the morning in question, Barry Brasher, using his own key, entered the Oleander pro shop for whatever reason. He apparently spotted in that barrel over there the left-handed wedge which had come in a couple of days before to be delivered to Corkney Clatter as a replacement for one he had broken. I believe that the Professor was not notified that it had arrived. Correct, Prof. Clatter?"

In a daze, Corkney could only nod agreement.

"Since a left-hander like Brasher doesn't get to see a great variety of clubs he can use, he apparently decided to try a swing or two with it. He was in his street shoes, and the footprints on the carpet show that he was standing with his back to this clothes rack."

Holding a left-handed club, I assumed a stance to imitate Brasher.

"You can see that there is room for a full swing of the club."

I demonstrated in my best left-handed fashion.

"But something happened to turn a routine practice swing into disaster. I believed it happened about like this."

At this point, I assumed the address position with my back very close to the clothes rack. After waggling the club, I shuffled my feet a couple of times as golfers do to get comfortable. I again settled into position, and in doing so my butt nudged the rack. Sure enough, that heavy metal bar swung silently out from the rack, at right angles to my stance and about four feet above the floor.

"At this point, Brasher didn't see that metal bar because he was concentrating on the imaginary golf ball on the imaginary tee in front of him. As he swung like this . . . except much harder than I am illustrating . . . he struck this heavy metal bar forcefully with his right wrist, crushing the bones severely. More importantly, the impact which so suddenly arrested his swing caused the club head to whip back. Since he was wearing smooth-soled loafers rather than golf spikes, his right foot slipped on the carpet, which made his head come up at an unusual angle . . . like this . . . causing the face of the club, as well as the leading edge, to make contact with his uplifted temple."

Everyone looked at me like Egyptian asps mesmerized by a particularly adept snake charmer. Not a word was said, so I continued.

"The wedge flew out of his hands upon impact, and sailed through the air about like this . . . landing on top of a bag of clubs positioned just where I've set that bag."

I was lucky, because my club toss landed right on target, and nestled among the heads of the clubs protruding from the substitute bag.

I continued. "A few minutes later, immediately after the body had been discovered, but before the police had arrived, the stock boy came in to put the bag of clubs into storage. The errant club was right on top of the bag, so without a second thought he inserted it into the bag with the others and took it to the locker room. (Incidentally, we have his deposition to that effect.) Only when he re-entered the pro shop did he see the body, panicked and ran away. Since the assistant pro who had discovered the body was in the men's room throwing up, no one knew to notify the police that something had been removed from the scene before they arrived."

I ended my recital and indicated that Lieutenant Tolliver and I would be glad to answer questions. Not surprisingly, the first questions came from Claude Cobra, who couldn't accept that we just might have done something right.

"A very interesting tale, well told, but just a tale nevertheless. Why should we believe it happened as you say?

B.B. spoke up, "The human tissue on the wedge, identified by DNA analysis as Brasher's, proves that it was the fatal instrument. The fingerprints on the club handle show that it was

169

Brasher who wielded it. To me, that's pretty convincing evidence that Brasher, and no one else, killed Brasher. That's the most important point as far as Law and Justice are concerned."

The Assistant D.A. couldn't think of a rebuttal, and subsided in his chair.

B.B. went on. "Still, we couldn't be satisfied with just that fact. If we are to sleep soundly, we need to know how things happen. Fortunately, DNA analysis of bits of tissue on this steel bar protruding from the clothes rack, proved that it was struck by Brasher's wrist. It's pretty hard to come up with a scenario other than Trebor gave you to explain that."

The coroner, who had not uttered a single word up to this point, stood up. "I have no problem with that," he intoned, put on his hat and walked out the door.

That was good news, because if the death was ruled to be accidental, the D.A. wasn't going to let Cobra or anyone else in his department waste time trying to prove otherwise.

Even Captain Frost allowed himself a modest smile. "Lieutenant Tolliver, this was great work, and I think you're in line for a commendation. Our thanks to you as well, Mr. Trebor. Now, can you explain to all of us what caused you to pursue the unusual idea that Brasher had killed himself?"

Billy Bob nodded to me to take the floor.

"The first point is that, while I'm doing most of the talking here, Lieutenant Tolliver and his people did most of the work and deserve the credit. But to address your question: we encountered several circumstances that didn't seem logical, so we tried to write a script in which they would make sense.

"For example, it didn't seem too likely that a murderer could have escaped through the side door of the shop without being seen through the windows by Mr. Flatbelly at the front door.

"Then there was the confined area between the large glass case and the clothes rack where the violence presumably occurred. There just wasn't sufficient room for one person to swing a golf club and strike another in that small space.

"Another puzzler was the pattern of footprints in the carpet. It was plain that Brasher's right foot, in street shoes, had slipped out from under him, probably because of the blow he absorbed. But the only other prints were made by golf spikes, and were quite faint and level, as would be made by walking and standing, not by vigorous action. As you can demonstrate for yourself, it doesn't take much effort to make quite a mark in this nappy carpet.

"Nor could we imagine what kind of a swing would be required to allow the face of a sharply-angled wedge to contact the victim's head in such a way.

"Meanwhile, we were diverted by the circumstantial evidence accumulating against Prof. Clatter: his hatred of Brasher, his lack of an alibi, the fact that he was left-handed and used the type of square-grooved clubs involved in the killing. And lastly, the fact that his wedge was missing from his bag."

Before I could continue Corkney let out a snort, "You were all ready to frame me!"

Captain Frost immediately squelched him. "Seems to me just the opposite is true. They had a strong case against you, but went that extra mile to pin down the truth instead. Go on, Mr. Trebor."

"Thank you. Brasher's footprints intrigued us, in that they seemed to be positioned for a golf swing. Even the mark showing the right foot dragging on the carpet was typical of the follow-through of an extremely fast swing. But when we learned that a left-handed club was involved, we abandoned this line of thought, assuming that Brasher was right-handed like almost everyone else, and wouldn't have swung a left-handed club. It was only later, in restudying the photo of the victim lying on the carpet, that we realized the golf glove was on the right hand, indicating that he was left-handed. This revelation caused us to pursue this approach in earnest.

"It was then that I revisited the scene, and discovered the phenomenon of the iron bar which floated out from the clothes rack, as you have observed. With that, we were able to postulate what had happened. Identification of microscopic bits of flesh on the bar as belonging to Brasher confirmed it."

Captain Frost broke in, "But how did you know where to look for the missing weapon?"

"Good question. Lieutenant Tolliver and I were convinced we had scripted the right scene. If this were true, then the weapon had to have been removed before the police arrived on the scene. We set about learning everything we could about the operation of the pro shop. Fortunately we ran across the routine of recording and storing golf bags for absent members. Following up on this with Ms. Nobley and the stock boy revealed that the latter had indeed removed a bag from the shop after the death but before the police arrived. As it turned out, the weapon was found in that bag."

There ensued a number of questions about details, which Lieutenant Tolliver answered effectively. While this was going on, I began to watch the two women. They were engaged in animated conversation, and it became embarrassingly obvious that I was the subject. I was gratified to see an occasional smile between them, finally followed by Fiona's melodious laugh and a hearty guffaw from Dorothy. Then they looked over at me, and Dorothy gave a 'thumbs up' sign. That was encouraging enough, but when Fiona winked at me and smiled I knew everything was right again.

About then Captain Frost broke up the party by asking me to accompany him and Billy Bob back to headquarters for an extended de-briefing. I walked over to Fiona to tell her the news.

"But Clive, I was hoping we might have tonight together."

"You and me both," I said fervently but ungrammatically, "But they can't keep me there *all* night!"

She smiled. "I'll keep the coffee pot warm," she said.

17.

I thought I'd never live to see Billy Bob Tolliver wearing white shirt, jacket and tie, much less sitting sedately in one of Savannah's finest eating establishments, where the specials weren't likely to include king-sized cheeseburgers and fat pork ribs. But there he was, in this ancient building housing the restaurant '1790', discussing the wine list with the sommelier, before ordering for his three guests.

The way this came about was that B.B.'s boss, Captain Frost, had made plenty of hay over the bizarre solution to the 'murder' of Barry Brasher, while Assistant D.A. Cobra had sulked a bit too long, and had missed out entirely on all the newspaper and television coverage. Quite a bit of the credit for this 'ingenious and inspired' police work, as the Press called it, landed in Lt. Tolliver's deserving lap. As any savvy politician would do, Frost went with the flow, and wangled a commendation and hefty pay raise for his subordinate.

As for me, I could see that the less anyone knew about my part in the investigation the better. I did manage to get some of the more questionable items in my expense account approved, along with an extension of the consulting arrangement until I lined up something else.

B.B. was uneasy that I hadn't received the recognition he thought I deserved, and as a token of appreciation, he invited me and my guests to any restaurant in town. I toyed with the idea of inviting all the barflies I'd gotten to know, along with Mary Alice Nobley, but decided it would be more fun with just Billy Bob, Fiona and me.

I put this proposal to Fiona, and she surprised me by asking if it was OK to bring along Dorothy LaMoste. What could I do? I was pretty sure that Dorothy wouldn't say anything to embarrass me, so I figured I could handle it.

After we had all ordered our dinner selections, Fiona stood up and proposed a toast: "Here's to Savannah's newest and finest interior design firm, and to my new partner, Dorothy LaMoste."

I started asking all kinds of questions, but what it boiled down to was that Dorothy was sick of her work in Narcotics, and Fiona was looking for a job in 'real life.' They both felt that they had found the answer.

So Billy Bob was basking in the security of a job he loved, and the two women were anticipating a glorious future in their newly chosen field, but what about old Clive? All of a sudden I felt like the little waif sitting in the rubble on one of those charity posters. No one spoke up, but their sympathy was obvious and embarrassing.

Finally B.B. broke the silence. "Clive, I reckon you're going to have a happy hunting grounds out there at the Soundings. Seems like there ought to be enough pigeons on all those golf courses to keep you busy seven days a week."

I didn't answer right away, but it occurred to me that Billy Bob was right. Still, for some reason I couldn't muster any enthusiasm for the prospect. Then all at once, I knew what was gnawing at me and how to fix it. Saying it out loud would commit me to it. I took a deep breath and went for it.

"Well, Old Partner, I don't mind taking a little cash from tourists and strangers, but I wouldn't feel right doing it to my new neighbors."

Fiona said, "Don't tell me the wandering Mr. Trebor is going to settle down!" There was surprise and happiness in her voice.

"Well," I said seriously, "I can't think of any better place to do it. The woman I love will be there, (a smirk at Fiona), along with good friends, (a smile for Dorothy), and it's about the nearest place to the Garden of Eden I've run across. Remember, there *still* has never been a serious crime committed on that island."

"What do you plan to do?"

"I've got several irons in the fire. For one, the Developer of The Soundings was very grateful that we protected their spotless image by proving that no crime had been committed on their sacred soil. He thinks that my investigative experience along with my golfing ability will be a good combination for a job he has in mind. We'll see."

The three of them began to tell me how great it was that we'd all be so close together. Each one in turn offered a toast to happiness and the future and such like. Then it was my turn.

I raised my glass of that exquisite Pouilly Fuisse we had talked our host into ordering.

"My toast," I said, "is a dual one. First a sincere one to Dan Dunn, who predicted there was a good chance that the killer would use a weapon he was most familiar with. Turned out he was right, although not in a way that any of us would have imagined. B.B., would you please thank him for us."

Billy Bob nodded agreement.

"The second toast," I went on, "is to the Goddess of Irony, if there be such a deity. Corkney Clatter threatened to kill Brasher personally, but ended up doing it by proxy, in the form of his own wanton wedge. His innocent action in ordering a new golf club ended up being responsible for his enemy's death."

We all drank to that, and about that time the waiter brought the appetizers. I was pleased to see that Billy Bob had already scarfed up all the rolls in the basket. For awhile there, I was afraid he'd gone wimpy on me.